SAVING DAMARIS

Saving Damaris

LAURA LEONARD

❧❧❧❧❧

A Jean Karl Book

ATHENEUM   1989   NEW YORK

Atheneum
Macmillan Publishing Company
866 Third Avenue, New York, NY 10022
Collier Macmillan Canada, Inc.
First Edition
Printed in the United States of America
Designed by Trish Parcell Watts
10 9 8 7 6 5 4 3 2 1

Library of Congress Cataloging-in-Publication Data
Leonard, Laura.
Saving Damaris/by Laura Leonard.
—1st ed.   p.   cm.
"A Jean Karl book."
Summary: In 1904, left destitute by the sudden death of their
mother and the continued absence of their father, twelve-year-old
Abby and her fourteen-year-old brother, Joel, try to find a way of
preventing their older sister from marrying, for the good of the
family, the very rich but unsuitable Mr. Buttchenbacher.
ISBN 0–689–31553–8
[1. Family problems—Fiction. 2. Brothers and sisters—Fiction.
3. Death—Fiction.] I. Title.
PZ7.L5485Sav   1989   [Fic]—dc19
89–6717   CIP   AC

To Ella Thorp Ellis,
with many thanks for her encouragement

SAVING DAMARIS

CHAPTER 1

❦❦❦❦❦

July 4, 1904

Excitement began to fizz up inside me the minute I opened my eyes. I pulled the sheet up to my chin and wriggled my toes against the footboard. It was the Fourth of July and my birthday!

My sister, Damaris, was already up and her bed neatly made. I snuggled back and watched the bits of light shine through speckled holes in our old, green window shade.

Mama lets us sleep as late as we want on our birthdays. That's why no one had called me.

The smell of bacon frying floated upstairs, and I heard Mama laugh. That made me feel good, too. Mama hasn't been laughing much lately. She doesn't when she's feeling poorly or worrying about Papa.

Suddenly a horrible, horrendous string of firecrackers went off practically under my window, and the dogs all up and down Lindstrom Street started barking their heads off.

"Joel!" I thought, jumping up. Dogs do not like the Fourth of July. Boys do. That includes my brother.

I scrambled over to the window, barefoot, not bothering with a wrapper. Sure enough there was Joel. He grinned up at me, long and thin as a stork and looking, as our uncle George says, "like a yard of pump water."

"Happy birthday, Baby Sister," he said.

"I'm not your *baby* sister!"

"That's right," he said, as though he had just remembered. "This is the great day, isn't it? Happy *twelfth* birthday, Sis."

Then, to my most horrible embarrassment, Joel's friend Luke Trabert stuck his head out from under the porch and said, "Happy birthday, Abby."

Luke is three years older than Joel and practically grown-up, being seventeen and already out of school and working for Mr. Ames, the photographer. And there I was, standing in the window in my nightgown!

I should have said thanks and shut the window. Instead, I said the first dumb thing that popped into my mouth, which was, "You better be careful you don't blow your head off, Joel Ezra Amos Edwards!"

I knew that Ezra Amos was a mistake as soon as I said it, though Joel just grinned again and said, "There's sliced peaches for breakfast. If you're planning on staying in bed all day . . . "

"I'm not."

"If you are, I'll be glad to eat your share, Miss *Abigail Keturah* Edwards," he said, getting even for that Ezra and Amos.

"I'll be right down," I said.

"Abigail Keturah?" Luke's eyebrows shot up about two miles.

"It comes from the Bible," I said. And then I slammed down the window.

Having a name like Abigail Keturah Edwards is a great trial. I plan to change it when I am a famous artist or an author like Mrs. Harriet Beecher Stowe or Louisa May Alcott. I haven't decided just what I'll change it to yet. The Edwards part is all right. It's just Abigail Keturah I can't stand.

At breakfast Joel asked what we were going to have for supper, and Mama said, "Abby gets to choose since she's the birthday child. . . . "

Then Joel winked and said, "I expect I better go out and pull up a big bunch of carrots for her."

"Don't bother on my account!" I said.

When I was a little kid before we moved to Estes and when Papa still lived with us most of the time, he mixed carrots up with my mashed potatoes, which were at the time my very favorite food in the world, and made me eat every single bite. I've never much liked carrots since, as Joel very well knows.

Mama told Joel not to tease. Then she gave me my birthday present. It was in a little package, wrapped in tissue and tied with a pink ribbon.

I was sure it was the ring I'd seen for sale at the Emporium, the one with a blue stone set in three kinds of gold: red, yellow, and green. I never knew there *were* three kinds of gold, even though Papa was a miner for years and years. Of course he never got to bring home samples.

"Happy birthday, darling," she said as she handed me the package. I thought it was that ring I'd been admiring for months and months, but it wasn't. It was a ring all right, but not that one.

"Thank you, Mama." I only hesitated just the littlest minute, so I don't think she knew I was the least bit disappointed. "I really wanted a ring."

"I know. I saw you looking at that one in the Emporium. This one belonged to my mother."

She pressed her hand up against her chest, so I knew she had that indigestion pain again. She says sometimes it hits her like an ice pick, and if she knew what she was eating that caused it, she surely would stop as it makes her weak as a kitten.

Her eyes looked a little anxious, so I said as quick as I could, "It's real pretty," and her forehead smoothed out.

It is a very nice ring. It's gold (plain yellow gold) with five little opals. Opals are sort of like pearls mixed with rainbows.

I know Mama thinks a lot of it. She has always worn it to church and the Ladies' Aid meetings, so I couldn't very well tell her I'd rather have had the other one.

Later Damaris said, "That's much nicer than the one down at the Emporium, Abby. The stones are real."

Everyone says Damaris is a real beauty. That's another hard thing, to have a sister who is a real beauty when you aren't. Sometimes I feel as if nobody sees me, they're all too busy looking at Damaris.

Mama says, "Be patient, Abby, your time will come." I don't think I will ever be as pretty as Damaris, even when my time comes.

Mama gave Damaris a ring on her twelfth birthday, four years ago, a store-bought ring. I guess she didn't have enough money to buy me one because Papa hasn't been able to send home much this year.

Last month was Joel's birthday. He wanted a new watch the worst way. Mama gave him an old one of Papa's. I think he was disappointed, too, though he didn't ever say.

Mama says we mustn't worry Papa about money. We can manage all right on what she makes sewing, especially now that Damaris is to start work down at the Emporium.

Joel bought me a set of drawing pencils, the very best quality, with money he's earned this summer, sweeping and taking tickets down at the railroad station. He'd rather be working on those big steam engines. Mama says he's "infatuated with grease." He gives most of what he makes to her. The extra money comes in real handy, but Mama says he'll have to give up the job when school starts.

Both our parents think a lot of schooling. That's how come we live in Estes, Kansas, Mama's old hometown. We moved here when I was three and Damaris really needed to go to school. Before that we followed Papa around to different mining camps, and Mama taught Damaris some at home. When Papa couldn't find a job in Estes, he had to go back to mining. He comes home when he can, which hasn't been often lately.

Damaris gave me a box of chocolate creams, which she knows I adore. She gave them to me yesterday so I wouldn't have to share with everybody today. She told me not to make myself sick eating them all at once, and I am resolved to eat only one a day. Maybe two.

Nothing has come from Papa. Mama put his name on the card with the ring, but I know he forgot.

I try not to let on to Mama that I mind about him

forgetting. I think she suspects, though, and that's really why she kept her hand pressing her chest while we ate breakfast—and not the indigestion at all.

We had just finished eating when there was a knock at the door.

"Aunt Eunice," Joel said, looking out the window.

"I expect she's wanting to talk about our picnic supper," Mama said with a warning look at us.

Aunt Eunice isn't a blood relative at all but only married to Uncle George, who is. He's Mama's brother. I think Mama is always afraid we will say something rude and impolite to Aunt Eunice. I can't remember when we ever did. Except once when she told Mama I was awful dark and skinny and a throwback to some black-headed Swede. I whispered to Joel that she was skinny as a toothpick herself, and she heard and got mad at me.

Mama told me later I mustn't make personal remarks. I said Aunt Eunice made them to me and she's always saying something about Papa and his "bad luck," only she makes it sound like he has bad luck intentionally.

Mama said that was no excuse and it was different because Aunt Eunice was all grown-up. That doesn't seem fair, but I never said again—not where she could hear—that Aunt Eunice was skinny, though she is.

Aunt Eunice rattled the doorknob and called through the screen, "Yoo-hoo! Is anybody home? It's time all you slugabeds were up. . . ."

"Unhook the screen, Abby," Mama said, as another string of firecrackers went off, and the dogs all up and down Lindstrom Street had fits again.

"Good morning, Emily," Aunt Eunice said. "Happy birthday, Abigail."

"Can I get you a cup of coffee, Eunice?" Mama already had the big gray graniteware pot in her hand, since Aunt Eunice has never been known to turn down a cup in her life.

"Might as well." Aunt Eunice put her hands over her ears, as another string of firecrackers went off outside. "There ought to be a law against fireworks, if you ask me. And listen to those animals! I didn't know there were that many dogs in town, much less on Lindstrom Street!"

Lindstrom Street was named for Mama's grandpa on her mother's side. He was Swedish. I guess that's why there are so many blonds in our family, though I'm not one myself.

And that's why we go to the Lutheran church. Uncle George says our Swedish blood is getting pretty diluted now. Great-grandpa Lindstrom was the last pure Swede in our family. Most all of the Swedish and German people in town are light haired and go to the Lutheran church, though Joel, who is always thinking of his stomach, says the Methodists have better pie socials.

Another string of firecrackers went off down at the

end of the street. Aunt Eunice put her hands over her ears again and said, "It's enough to make a body jump right out of their skin."

"It's only one day a year," Mama said.

"Thank fortune for that! I just came down to tell you not to bother with the chicken for tonight's picnic. I've fried up plenty for all of us."

"Thank you, Eunice. Your fried chicken is always a treat." Then Mama turned to me and said, "Abby, you may be excused, if you like."

"What? With all those breakfast dishes left to do?" That was Aunt Eunice who said that, of course.

Mama smiled at me. "We'll let her off this morning since she's the birthday child."

"I declare. You'll spoil her, Emily."

"Birthdays are special," Mama said. "Go along and see if Dolly is coming to your picnic supper, Abby."

Dolly Raymond is my best friend in the world. We always go to each other's birthday parties, only Dolly doesn't have to invite all her relations to come to hers the way I do.

"I don't suppose Abigail has heard from her father," Aunt Eunice said, as I slid out of my chair and headed toward the door.

"Not yet," said Mama.

"And won't, most likely. You'd think the man could remember the child's birthday."

"John's been busy. . . . " Mama put her hand up against her chest, so I knew she had that indigestion pain again.

"Is he still chasing fool's gold in Alaska?"

"No," Mama said, her lips getting tight.

Papa is in Sacramento, California, as Aunt Eunice very well knows. He is starting a new job with the U.S. Geological Survey. We hope this one works out better than the mining.

"Humph," Aunt Eunice said, as if it was something she could chop off with a hatchet. Her nose twisted up as though she smelled something purely dreadful, like a dead rat. "It's always something with John Edwards. Hasn't sent you a red cent for months, has he? Has he even written?"

I slipped out to the veranda, not wanting to hear Aunt Eunice go on about Papa and his bad luck again.

Papa *has* had a run of bad luck. Last spring he got pneumonia and lost his job at that mercury mine near Clear Lake in California. The year before, he broke his leg and the company he worked for went broke. That's why Mama has to take in sewing to make ends meet.

He didn't much like it at the mercury mine. He wrote that it was no fit place for a family, with "no church, no school, but plenty of rattlesnakes."

It was getting hot on the veranda. The sky was a pale, cloudless blue. I wriggled back into the shade, where it was still cool.

I know I'm not Papa's favorite. He never called me

Princess, the way he did Damaris. And I know he's busy. But wouldn't you think, with all the fireworks and celebrations to remind him, he could at least remember when I was born?

CHAPTER 2

✦✦✦✦✦

Tuesday, July 5

It turned out to be a lovely birthday, one of the best I ever had. Well, it was mostly a lovely birthday.

After the Independence Day parade and after all the singing and band music and speechifying was done, we had our picnic supper. Besides the fried chicken, we had potato salad, pickles, sliced tomatoes, lemonade, and, for dessert, my favorite . . . angel food cake.

Joel said, "What do you mean your favorite? All desserts are your favorite." I do have a terrible sweet tooth. Joel says I may be skinny now but I'm going to end up looking like Mrs. Smith Kenyon, who lives down the street. She calls herself "pleasingly plump," which Joel says is half right. I like Mrs. Smith Kenyon, but she is plump, all right.

Dolly Raymond did come to our picnic supper. So did Joel's friend Luke and, of course, so did Aunt Eunice, Uncle George, and the little boys. The little boys were pretty good this year. Last year Clay broke his arm, and Delbert fell on the cake.

We always have to invite them all. Mama says she doesn't know how she could have managed without Uncle George, with Papa gone so much. Joel can do most of the small jobs, but when something big needs fixing and Papa's not around (which is almost always), Uncle George sees to it.

Mama keeps quarters and dimes in an old brown teapot high up on a kitchen shelf. If her sewing jobs slack off and the teapot gets really empty, Uncle George is sure to show up lugging a sack of flour or cornmeal, or some of Daisy's good butter. Daisy is their cow. Uncle George says Aunt Eunice'd sooner give up him than Daisy, she thinks that much of that cow, but I don't really think that's so.

Before our picnic supper Uncle George slipped a dollar

in my pocket, like he used to do lemon drops when I was little.

"Buy something pretty for yourself," he said, but I think I will save it for something really nice for Mama at Christmas. I thanked him and said he was my favorite uncle.

He laughed and said, "I'm your *only* uncle," which is the truth. Then supper was ready, and he said we better get ours or there wouldn't be anything left for the birthday girl. Everything was absolutely delicious. Aunt Eunice's chicken was crisp and crunchy and the angel food cake light as a cloud. I ate until I was positively stuffed. Dolly said she was, too.

After supper, while Damaris was sitting on the porch talking to Luke, Mr. Buttchenbacher, who has hired her to work down at the Emporium, drove by in his buggy and tipped his hat to her.

Damaris looked real pretty in her white muslin dress. She never seems to get grass stains or grease spots or to spill anything on her clothes ever.

Dolly Raymond poked me in the ribs. Then she whispered in my ear, "I bet Luke Trabert is sweet on Damaris," which is real ridiculous.

"Luke comes to see Joel," I said. "They've been friends practically forever." I was already feeling cross with Dolly because she had asked what Papa had sent me, and I had had to say nothing.

"Of course," Dolly went on, as though I hadn't said a word, "it will be just years and years before Luke can support a wife."

"A wife! Damaris is too young to get married to *anybody*!"

"She's sixteen, isn't she? That's plenty old enough to start looking around. Being as she's so pretty, I expect she won't be working down at the Emporium very long. . . . Did you notice how Mr. Buttchenbacher looked at her?"

"Now you are being ridiculous, Dolly!"

"Well, he is probably too old for her."

"I should say so!"

"All the same, I bet Damaris will be getting married to somebody right soon. Ma says that's the only fitting thing for a girl to do, anyway."

"Well," I said, really upset, "*my* mother says a brain is a brain whether it's male or female, and the only *fitting* thing is to use it the best we can. And getting married has nothing to do with *that*!"

"My, you do get excited over nothing, Abby. It's not like you have to leap in and save Damaris from some awful fate! What else is a girl supposed to do besides get married? Turn into an old-maid schoolteacher?"

"Lots of things!"

"Like what?"

"There are lady doctors and nurses and that Madame

Curie in Paris. . . . She won the Nobel Prize for physics last year. . . . "

"You mean you'd like to do such nasty stuff as cleaning up after sick people. And my goodness, medical students have to cut up *cadavers*! You wouldn't catch me doing that in a million years!" Dolly shuddered. Dr. Raymond is her daddy, so I guess she knows about such things.

"I wouldn't mind," I said.

"You wouldn't!"

"Well, maybe I would, but if I wanted to be a doctor, I'd go ahead and do it, though, of course, I won't have to since I plan to be an artist or an author. . . . "

How is it that no sooner do you get mad at somebody than they do something nice and then you feel like two measly cents? It happens sometimes with Aunt Eunice (but not very often). And it happened right then with Dolly. There I was getting mad enough to burst, when she goes and gives me a birthday present, a brand-new notebook.

"I know you've almost filled up that little old ledger you scribble in," she said, "and I didn't want you to go blind writing crossways in it. . . . "

I've been using an old ledger of Papa's for my diary. It has his name inside the cover. John Malcolm Edwards. It belonged to him when he was young and learning to be a bookkeeper, before he married Mama and went out West to try his hand at mining.

With money being scarce, I haven't wanted to ask for a new notebook. When I filled the ledger up, I planned to start over at right angles across what I wrote before. People used to do that in letters to save on postage, but it is hard to read, so I really appreciated Dolly's present.

"Thank you, Dolly," I said, and put my arms around her. "It's just what I needed."

And we both got sort of blubbery-eyed and promised faithfully we would always be friends and would never, ever argue about anything again.

After supper we watched the fireworks at the park. Later Joel and Luke Trabert set off some at home. Aunt Eunice kept saying that firecrackers are dangerous, that she would never allow *her* boys to touch them, and that Joel would likely blow off a couple of fingers.

Uncle George said, "Eunice, don't you go to worrying Emily. Joel and Luke are careful. It's good to see Joel act like a boy for a change. He gets little enough chance these days."

I don't think Mama liked his saying that, though she's always saying herself how Joel has to be the man of the house, with Papa gone so much of the time.

Joel and Luke were careful and didn't blow anything off, I'm glad to say.

At nine o'clock Uncle George yawned and asked Mama to play a tune on the piano. Mama said she wasn't really up to it. She looked awfully pale, but she said she was just tired. Damaris played instead and sang "Sylvia" and "I Dreamt I Dwelt in Marble Halls," because they are my favorites. Then Dolly's pa came for her, and everybody went home. Joel had to help carry home the little boys. Dennis, Delbert, and Stewart were like three sacks of potatoes. Only Clay managed it on his own two feet.

Mama came up to my room after everyone was gone and sat down on the edge of my bed. "I hope you had a nice birthday, Abby," she said.

"Perfect." I turned my ring so the opals caught fire in the lamplight. "If only . . . "

"If only what, Abby?"

I bit my lips, sorry I said anything. "It was just Dolly. She asked . . . "

"What Papa sent?" she said, and I nodded.

Mama pushed the hair back from my eyes. She has the prettiest hands. They're soft and pale. She wears gloves when she works in the kitchen or the yard so they won't get rough. That's because when she takes in sewing she doesn't want to fray her customers' material. Her nails are so pale they look almost blue. My hands are positively red next to hers. I have tried to draw hers, but it's hard because they are never still.

"It's just that Dolly's pa always remembers. . . . "

"You mustn't mind about not hearing from Papa. He's working hard so we can all be together. And besides, men just don't always remember things like birthdays on their own. Dr. Raymond has Dolly's mama right there to remind him."

She pressed her hand hard against her chest. It makes me feel bad when she does that. I reached up and hugged her tight.

"There, Abby," she said, pushing back my hair. "One of these days Papa will have a job in a regular town with proper schools and churches, and then he'll send for us. And we will be sure to remind him of important dates like twelfth birthdays. . . . "

Then I went to sleep and dreamed of Papa. His hair was gold like Damaris's is in lamplight . . . and he called *me* Princess. I woke up wondering if Papa will ever send for us . . . or if I really want him to.

CHAPTER 3

※-※-※-※-※

Wednesday, July 6

This was Damaris's first day at the Emporium. She got up (and woke me up) practically at the crack of dawn.

Well, I guess it wasn't exactly that early because Mama was already up and at the sewing machine. I stuck the pillow over my head and tried to ignore the sound of the treadle and go back to sleep, but it was no use.

Damaris has been putting up her hair for ages, ever

since she started business school, but she couldn't seem to do it up to suit herself this morning. She kept sighing and fussing until I said, "It looks all right to me."

"All right isn't good enough," she said. "Not today."

"It looks fine."

"Does it? It's hard to tell with this mirror. It's really awful." The mirror is an old one Aunt Eunice gave us. It's small and sort of greenish with brown spots where the silver's gone in back.

"Maybe now that I'll be working I can save up for a new one," she said, still frowning at her reflection.

There's no end to the things Damaris wants to get, now that she's working. Aunt Eunice says her first paycheck is going to melt faster than a snowball in August.

She pinned on her hat, took one last look, and said, "Well, I guess that will have to do. I don't want to be late my first day."

Mama was proud of Damaris when she graduated so young from Mr. Perkins's Business School. Mr. Perkins himself congratulated her. He said her shorthand couldn't be distinguished from the example in Mr. Gregg's book and that she should have no trouble finding a job as a fully qualified stenographer.

He was wrong about that, though. The only job she was able to find was down at the Emporium, selling ribbons and yardage.

Before she left, Damaris sat down on the edge of the

bed next to me and said, "Abby, Mama has been working awfully hard. I wish she'd turn down some of this work."

"She won't," I said.

"No, I don't suppose she will." Damaris frowned. "You will help her while I'm gone, won't you, Abby?"

"Of course." She didn't have to tell me how to behave. After all, I'm not a baby. I must have sounded cross. I guess that made her think I didn't want to help.

"It won't be that bad, Abby."

"Not unless I have to cook," I said with a sigh. "You know what Joel says."

"He likes to tease."

What Joel says is, "Oh, Abby can cook all right if you don't mind rubbery eggs and burned toast." And the trouble is, that's mostly the truth.

"What if I buy you a cookery book of your very own, Abby, now that I'm working?" Damaris asked.

I said that was very nice of her, but I wasn't sure it would do any good. When you cook, you have to get everything done at the same time, and I don't think any old book can tell you how. Damaris said not to worry because she would help when she got home from the Emporium.

Thursday, July 7

I tried to make a sponge cake today. It came out one-half inch high. I forgot the baking powder. You'd think I could learn to cook, much as I like eating.

When I was little I used to rate people by what they had to eat (and gave us). Joel found out, and he's never let me forget it. I'm afraid sometime he'll tell Mama I used to call Aunt Eunice "Mrs. Bread Pudding," because we had it a lot when we stayed there. That was when we first came back to Estes before we had our own place. I guess it will serve me right if I never learn to cook!

Dolly's ma was always the "Dessert Lady." She makes an elegant lime pie and a heavenly Lady Baltimore cake with inch-thick frosting all decorated with almonds and slivers of candied apricot. Mama cooks best of all. She can make even eggs and greens taste good, when we're running short on money.

Friday, July 8

This afternoon I went to Dolly's house. Mrs. Raymond had company. She was serving tea and a chocolate torte with whipped cream. *Torte* is a fancy name for a cake.

Dolly says her ma does the baking herself. She does it early in the morning, and her kitchen has to be as spotless as Dr. Raymond's surgery.

The surgery is what Dr. Raymond calls the room he has all fitted up with the interesting-looking instruments he uses when he has to sew up cuts or fix broken legs.

Or when kids stick beans up their noses. Junior Smith Kenyon did that once.

I've never seen Mrs. Raymond with so much as a smudge of flour on her face. She always looks like she came out of the Emporium's display window. Dolly says it's a great trial to live with people who are so keen on spit and polish and scrubbing up as her folks, especially if you aren't especially neat, which Dolly isn't, though she tries.

Mrs. Raymond told Dolly we should go to the kitchen and ask the "maid" for some of the chocolate torte.

The "maid" is Bridget Malone. Aunt Eunice says Mrs. Raymond is putting on airs, that Bridget is just a plain hired girl, though Dolly's ma makes her wear a dark dress and a white cap and apron when there are guests and won't let her eat at the table with the family.

As Dolly and I went up to her room, we heard Mrs. Raymond tell her visitors she was afraid Bridget was a bad influence because she reads "trashy romances" and "cheap novels."

"When does Bridget have time to read?" I asked. It seemed to me Dolly's ma kept her pretty busy scrubbing and polishing.

"She has half an hour at lunch. The books aren't trash. That is, Bridget says the books aren't trash at all but real interesting stories. She orders them from Sears and Roebuck the same as Joel does his electricians' and engineers' handbooks. There's some by Mrs. Bertha M. Clay she likes real well."

"Have you read them?" I asked.

"Mama doesn't want me to," she said, which wasn't exactly answering my question. "I bet you could write one, Abby. Maybe when you're older you can write something as good as Mrs. Clay's *A Woman's Mistake* or *Orange Blossoms and Thorns.*"

I *know* Dolly has read those books or else how would she know the titles? Besides, she got all pink and looked awfully guilty.

"You could just make piles of money," Dolly said. I was busy thinking what all I could do with piles of money when she said, "Then your mama wouldn't have to take in sewing and Damaris wouldn't have to work down at the Emporium and Joel could go to college like he wants to. . . . "

"How do you know that?" I demanded, plenty aggravated.

"Don't get upset with me, Abigail Edwards. Everybody in town knows your mama is having a hard time."

"You don't have to talk about it, Dolly Raymond!" I said, trying not to lose my temper. It makes you feel *positively naked* to find out that everybody in town knows all your business and talks about it to everybody else.

Dolly held out the plate of chocolate torte to me (which I ignored) and said, "My mother says if your papa was to send for you all or send you enough money, none of you would have to work. Then you wouldn't need to become a great writer at all."

"He'll probably be sending for us any day now," I said, which Dolly probably didn't believe because I didn't myself.

"I didn't mean to upset you, Abby." Dolly put her arms around me. "I hope your papa doesn't send for you. I hope you never ever have to leave Estes!"

That made me feel a little better, though I was still some put out and went home without eating another piece of Mrs. Raymond's elegant-tasting torte.

As I walked home, I scuffed along in the dust and thought about writing books. I'd just turned the corner to our street when a carriage passed. I looked up and saw Damaris sitting beside Mr. Karl Buttchenbacher.

Mr. Buttchenbacher goes to the Lutheran church, the same as we do. He smells of bay rum and smokes cigars, the fifty-cent kind, and owns the Estes Emporium, where Damaris works. I wondered how come he was bringing Damaris home.

Then I started thinking that if I could write and make a lot of money, then maybe Mama wouldn't have to work so hard, and we could afford a fancy carriage like Mr. Buttchenbacher's.

I do make up stories for the little Smith Kenyons when I stay with them. It's the only way I can keep them quiet.

They like my stories, but I'm sure they wouldn't want anything like *Orange Blossoms and Thorns.* They'd rather have blood, guts, and train wrecks. And Junior Smith Kenyon would want something like *A Manual on the Dissection of Frogs, Rats, and Earthworms*—with lots of illustrations.

CHAPTER 4

※-※-※-※-※

Saturday, July 9

This morning I asked Damaris how she liked working down at the Emporium. She had her mouth full of hair-pins so she couldn't answer right away.

Then she said, "It's all right. It's hard at first, starting something new, but it's all right."

"What's Mr. Buttchenbacher like?"

She hesitated a minute and then said, "He's been very kind."

Mr. Buttchenbacher doesn't look very kind, but then, everybody is kind to Damaris. I don't know whether it's because she's so pretty or because she's kind to them first. Damaris can be stubborn at times, but she mostly does have a good disposition. I think it must be easier to have a good disposition if you're pretty.

After she left, I tried to put my hair up. Caesar, the Smith Kenyons' big orange cat, jumped up on the windowsill and watched me out of those yellow-green eyes.

My hair slipped and slid and slithered. How do Mama and Damaris manage anyway? Caesar blinked, yawned, and left, and I took down the whole slippery mass and put it in two braids as usual.

This afternoon after I finished my chores, I sat out on the veranda and started to draw Caesar. He was curled up in the shade, making himself right at home, but when I took out my sketchbook, he opened one eye and looked at me suspiciously. I pretended I was drawing the big old cottonwood out back, so after a minute he closed his eyes and went back to sleep.

Cats are so graceful and elegant. If I had to be an animal, I think I would like to be a cat. Or maybe a bird—a hawk. It looks so easy the way they float up there in the summer sky. I don't much think I'd like to eat snakes and raw rabbits, though.

It's hard to see changes in light and shadow and shades of color. I'm trying to train my eye, but I don't know exactly how to go about it.

If I try to draw every hair on Caesar, every line can look like a perfect hair in the perfect place but my picture doesn't look a bit like Caesar. I've decided you have to know what to leave out as well as what to put in.

I was so busy drawing I didn't hear Mrs. Smith Kenyon come up the walk. I jumped about a mile when she laughed and said, "I see Caesar is here again. You folks aren't feeding him, are you?"

"No, ma'am," I said.

Mama came to the door then. They both said how hot it was, and Mama said as how the heat was bothering her more than usual this year.

Mrs. Smith Kenyon had brought over a christening dress for Mama to mend. She said it was an heirloom. Her sister in Kansas City had asked the loan of it for her youngest child. Mrs. Smith Kenyon wanted to take it with her when she went to visit her folks.

"But just look at it!" She held it up. There was a big hole in the lace. "One look at that, and Sally May would have my scalp. Our great-grandma made every stitch of it, lace and all."

Mama looked at the big hole and shook her head. "Such fine work," she said, "how did that hole happen anyway?"

"My Arthur, Arthur Junior, that is," she said with a laugh. "He found Myrna playing bride with it—as she shouldn't have been—using it for a veil, you know. He snatched it right off her head, and just see what happened. I know if anybody can fix this up, you can, Emily."

"I'll see what I can do."

"I sure appreciate it." Out of the corner of my eye, I saw Aunt Eunice come up the street toward us as she does most every afternoon. She was carrying the baby, Stewart, and the other three were trailing along behind.

As Mrs. Smith Kenyon turned to go, she looked at my drawing and said, "You and Mr. Edwards will have to think about sending this girl to art school, Emily."

Of course Aunt Eunice arrived just in time to hear her. She waited until Mrs. Smith Kenyon was out the gate. Then she sniffed and said, "What nonsense! Does she think that china painting she does makes her an art expert?"

"How are you, Eunice?" Mama said.

"Art school!" Aunt Eunice went on. "The woman's got straw for brains. How are you supposed to manage that? You've done well to keep them fed and clothed, as little help as you get from John. . . . "

Mama was getting that pinched look around her mouth. "I'll just go in and make us a nice pitcher of lemonade," she said. "That will really hit the spot today."

"You let Abby make the lemonade, Emily. She knows how, or if she don't she ought to. You look plumb tuckered out. George was asking just yesterday if you was off your feed."

Sometimes I think Aunt Eunice tries to get rid of me so she can talk to Mama in private. It didn't work this time. The window was open so I could hear every word she said while I squeezed the lemons. Not that most of it was anything I hadn't heard her say about eleventeen million times before.

She began with, "You're too easy on Abigail, Emily"—I made a face as I sliced the lemons—"Abigail's a dreamer. She's liable to turn out as shiftless as that Smith Kenyon woman. I hear *she's* going off again to visit her folks. I guess I'd do the same if George worked for the railroad and could get me a pass. I do pity her husband, though. Between her china painting and her gypsying around the countryside, it's a wonder the poor man has a clean pair of drawers to his name, though maybe he don't."

"Damaris and Joel have turned out all right. Abby will, too," Mama said, and that made me feel good.

"Well, you listen to me, Emily. You let Abby help and maybe you won't be looking like you was dragged through a knothole sideways."

When I took out the lemonade, Aunt Eunice was asking how Damaris was doing and if she liked working at the Emporium. Then she said Mr. Karl Buttchenbacher was "a fine man" and "good catch for somebody . . . Damaris maybe." She didn't seem to notice Mama's mouth getting that tight look on it.

"Now, Eunice—" Mama said.

"Don't you 'Now, Eunice' me, Emily. And don't pretend it wouldn't be a load off your mind if Damaris at least was to be settled down."

"I don't want her settled down before she has time to grow up, Eunice."

Then they had some more words, and Mama said she was thinking about her future when she let Damaris go to business school and she only hoped someone didn't marry her just because she has a pretty face.

Aunt Eunice said, "Well, it's lucky for Damaris she does have a pretty face. Men don't go around examining a girl's brain when they get in the marrying mood."

Then she said she had to be getting on home. Dennis and Delbert and Stewart were playing in the yard, but Clay had disappeared, and I was sent to find him. He was down at the Smith Kenyons'. He'd fallen down and skinned his knees, and Aunt Eunice about had a fit.

She would have had more of a fit if she'd been the one to find him. Junior Smith Kenyon had him tied to a tree, and he and Myrna and the twins were pretending they were going to scalp him. I *think* they were pretending. With the Smith Kenyons you never know.

When Aunt Eunice finally left, Mama sighed and said, "I guess a body wouldn't know they were ailing if Eunice didn't tell them so."

Her voice sounded sad. I looked up at her quickly, and she smiled at me and said, "Don't you let Aunt Eunice worry you, Abby. You're a big help, and I appreciate it."

That made me feel good. I snuggled up and put my arms around her. I have resolved to work my fingers clear down to the bone if I have to, to help Mama . . . and to show Aunt Eunice I'm not lazy.

CHAPTER 5

꙰꙰꙰꙰꙰

Sunday, July 10

Today I filled Aunt Eunice's sugar bowl with salt. I didn't mean to, but I expect it's another thing I will never live down.

After church Aunt Eunice and Uncle George asked us over for Sunday dinner. Mama said the heat was making her a bit faint and she believed she better go home, but Damaris, Joel, and I should go without her.

Then Aunt Eunice invited Pastor Needham and, of

all people, Damaris's boss, Mr. Buttchenbacher. He came over and lifted his hat to Damaris, started talking to Uncle George, and then Aunt Eunice had to go and invite him, too.

Aunt Eunice always calls Mr. Buttchenbacher a fine figure of a man. I can't see it myself. He certainly is substantial. There's quite a lot of front to him. He looks very clean and scrubbed, even his scalp. He has a lot of hair in front but a round bald spot in back. He takes soda mint pills for his stomach, and he has real shiny boots.

I think Damaris was embarrassed when Aunt Eunice invited him because she got all pink and didn't seem to know what to say. She looked relieved when Mrs. Smith Kenyon came bustling up and said, "Damaris, dear, has your mama gone already? I wanted to ask about her piano. I heard she was planning to sell it. . . . "

"It's not for sale, Mrs. Smith Kenyon," Damaris said.

Aunt Eunice who had been busy talking to Mr. Buttchenbacher turned right around and said, "Damaris, don't you go speaking for your mama." And then, "Althea, you talk to Emily. I know she's never wanted to part with it, but you ask Emily yourself. She just might have changed her mind. Circumstances are some different now and . . . "

Both Joel and Damaris looked embarrassed. I probably did, too, waiting for Aunt Eunice to say, as usual, "Beggars can't be choosers," which she did. Every time we start having money problems, Aunt Eunice is after Mama to sell the piano, but she won't.

Mama and Uncle George both got a small inheritance from some great-aunt I never met. The first thing Mama did, the only thing she did, was to go out and buy that piano. Uncle George put his into his hardware store.

"You can ask Mama, but I'm sure it's not for sale, Mrs. Smith Kenyon," Damaris said again.

"Let me know if it is, dear. I do want the children to take lessons. I hear that new Professor Vincent is taking pupils. My Junior and Myrna are quite musical, you know." Mrs. Smith Kenyon drifted off and gathered the six little Smith Kenyons around her like a plump, fluffy hen with a bunch of chicks, and we went off to Aunt Eunice and Uncle George's house.

It was while Aunt Eunice was dishing up dinner that she asked me to fill the sugar bowl and I filled it with salt by mistake.

When I'm eighty years old and Aunt Eunice is a hundred and ten, she will still be saying, "Remember that time Pastor Needham and Mr. Buttchenbacher came to dinner and Abigail filled the sugar bowl with salt?"

Monday, July 11

Today when I went to Dolly's, *her* mother asked about the piano.

"It's not for sale," I said.

"Do you play, Abigail?" Mrs. Raymond fixed those black eyes on me. They shine like shoe buttons.

"No," I said. "Damaris does."

Damaris has a nice voice, too. She wants to save her money now that she's working so she can have proper voice training.

"Your sister does have quite a nice little talent," Mrs. Raymond said. "Such a ladylike accomplishment. I don't know how your mother can permit her to go out to business."

"Mama says a girl should know how to support herself," I said.

"That is necessary, I suppose, when a man is not able to take proper care of his family. . . . "

Somehow Mrs. Raymond always manages to get me riled up. Dolly brought slices of her twelve-egg pound cake later for us to sample, but I was still so upset I didn't feel like eating a bite, but I did anyway to be polite.

Tuesday, July 12

Joel brought home an old broken-down bicycle he bought for a quarter from Mr. Avery Trabert. Mr. Trabert is Luke's uncle who works for the railroad, the one Luke calls a "big wheel." He's Mr. Smith Kenyon's boss.

Joel thinks he can repair the bicycle. Uncle George said he wouldn't be surprised if he fixes it up first-rate since Joel is mighty clever with his hands.

It's still hot. There's been heat lightning off to the west but not a drop of rain.

Mrs. Smith Kenyon paid me a dime for staying with the children while she went to the Methodist Church Rummage Sale. She ordinarily goes to the Lutheran church like we do, but she said a bargain is a bargain even if it is a Methodist bargain.

I took her the christening dress Mama mended. She was pleased with it and asked if Mama was real busy with sewing orders. She wants some school clothes for Junior and Myrna and a couple of other things done before she goes to visit her folks in Kansas City. Aunt Eunice says they go on a pass. I didn't exactly know what a pass was, so I asked Mrs. Smith Kenyon. It's a free ticket. Mr. Smith Kenyon has worked for the railroad for just years and years, so he gets one.

I sighed and said, "I expect if I ever want a ticket, I'll have to buy it unless they decide to let girls be engineers or conductors."

Mrs. Smith Kenyon laughed until her sides jiggled. "You might not have to wait that long. If Joel goes to work for the railroad permanently, not just summers, why I expect he could get a pass, too."

That did give me something to think about as I walked home. The rummage sale was still going on when I went past the Methodist church, so I stopped and bought a cookbook with my dime. Now Damaris won't have to get me one when she gets paid.

It's called *Mrs. Brown's Prize Receipt Book*. (*Receipt* is another word for recipe.) Maybe if I study it, Mama will let me cook. She says if I keep the house swept and picked up and get my other chores done, that's enough. I believe she thinks it's more work to tell me how to cook than to do it herself or to let Damaris do it.

I was sitting on the steps looking through the recipes when Joel came and sat beside me. I slid the book under my apron so he wouldn't see it. I didn't feel like being teased about my cooking, but I needn't have bothered because he didn't pay any attention. Caesar came up and rubbed against his leg. Joel patted him absently.

"Penny for your thoughts," I said.

"There's a job open at the telegraph office. I think I can get it. It's full-time starting next month."

"Mama won't *ever* let you quit school, Joel," I said. "Remember what happened last time."

In June before school was out Mr. Tobias Johnson, who has charge of maintaining the engines at the train yard, was willing to take Joel on as an apprentice. Luke's uncle recommended Joel. Joel wanted to take that job bad enough to spit because he dearly loves anything to do with engines, but he didn't know how to tell Mama.

I had what I thought was a *brilliant idea*.

I said, "Why not wait until Aunt Eunice gets here for afternoon coffee before you talk to Mama. She's always saying we should go to work. She'll be on your side for sure, and maybe she can talk Mama into it."

My idea wasn't much good. It wasn't any good at all. In fact it was *purely awful.*

Mama said, "No. Absolutely not."

Aunt Eunice told her it was a good opportunity for Joel. It didn't mean he was going to quit learning, for goodness' sake.

Mama still said, "No, absolutely not. I will not raise any ignorant, uneducated children."

"I suppose you call your own brother ignorant," Aunt Eunice said. You could tell she was all riled up.

"No, of course I don't," Mama tried to say, but Aunt Eunice just plowed right on. She said Uncle George was an educated man even though he only finished eighth grade. He had his own hardware business. He wasn't raising his children like a bunch of gypsies or a tribe of wild Indians while he pranced about all over the country hunting silver and gold.

" . . . Like some others I could name," she finished. Then she marched off in a huff, and Mama went to her room and shut the door.

Aunt Eunice and Mama didn't speak for a week after that, and I felt it was all my fault.

Down the street I heard Aunt Eunice call, "Stewie! come along. Let's go see Auntie Emily." The baby's name is Stewart, but she calls him Stewie. That's almost worse than Abigail Keturah or Ezra Amos put together.

"I guess you better not wait for Aunt Eunice to speak up for you this time, Joel," I said.

"No," he said, getting up. "I'll talk to Mama later. Aunt Eunice's help is worse than none at all."

CHAPTER 6

Wednesday, July 20

Today I am going to fix dinner all by myself. I've been planning it ever since I bought *Mrs. Brown's Prize Receipt Book* and today's the day!

Mama has been real busy sewing. Otherwise she might not have agreed. Mrs. Smith Kenyon ordered all those clothes for her children, and now Dolly's ma wants a new dress copied from a magazine picture. It's full of bows and pleats and little bitty tucks and gathers and looks awfully hard to do, but Mama can make almost anything.

"This will certainly keep me some busy," Mama said after Mrs. Raymond left, "but it will help with the rent." She got that little frown line between her eyes, and I knew she was thinking of Papa and wondering why we hadn't heard from him.

"Papa's sure to be all right," I said to make her feel better.

"Why, of course he is," she said. "I expect he just can't get to a post office, with all that traveling for the survey team."

I hope she's right.

This afternoon she has some errands to do down at the Emporium. As she was putting on her hat she said, "While I'm down there, I'll stop in and ask Doctor Raymond for some tonic. With all this work to be done, I have to keep up my strength."

That's when I said I'd cook dinner to help out. She looked doubtful and said, "Are you sure you want to do that all by yourself? Why not wait until I get home to help or Damaris does?"

"You let Damaris cook when she was twelve," I said.

"So I did. I forget you're almost grown, honey. It *will* be a big help if you cook dinner." Then she gave me a hug and asked, "What do you want to fix?"

"It's going to be a surprise."

"Well, don't try anything too complicated," she said as she went out the door.

I haven't planned anything complicated at all. Anybody can fix stew. I must have watched Mama do it a couple million times. All you do is throw everything in the pot to cook until, as Mrs. Brown says, the meat is "fork tender."

Maybe I will get a little bit fancy and look up the recipe for dumplings, but first I have to go to the butcher's and get a nice piece of stewing beef.

Thursday, July 21

Mama says everyone makes mistakes. That's how we learn.

I don't know why every time I make one, Aunt Eunice has to be right on the spot to see me do it.

Yesterday I peeled the potatoes and carrots. Carrots are all right when there's plenty of gravy to cover the taste. I built up the fire and put everything in a pot to cook.

After I hunted up the recipe for dumplings, I began to wonder if Mrs. Brown was going to be much help to me. All her recipes call for a pinch of this, a teacup of that, and lard the size of a hen's egg as though everybody's pinch, teacup and hen's eggs are the same size.

As it was almost four-thirty, I decided to forget about the dumplings. The stew had been cooking about an hour, and it sure was getting hot in the kitchen. I had just poked the meat to see if it was "fork tender" (which it wasn't) when who should put her head in the back door but Aunt Eunice.

"Yoo-hoo, Emily," she said, coming straight on in without waiting to be invited.

"Phew," she said, "it's hotter than Hades in here, Abby. Whatever is your ma doing in all this heat?"

"Mama's not here," I said.

"So I see. Where is she?"

"She went down to get some thread from the Emporium."

"Damaris ought to have done that, seeing as how she works there every livelong day. Your ma ought to learn how to manage her time better."

"She had to get some tonic anyway," I said.

"From Doc Raymond?" I nodded, and then she said without even stopping for breath, "Whatever have you got in that pot, Abby?"

"Stew."

So then she takes off the lid and sticks a fork in the beef. She looked at the clock and said, "When did you expect this to be ready, Abby? Not for dinner, I hope."

I didn't know (and Mrs. Brown hadn't mentioned) that *stew meat* has to be cooked practically forever to be "fork tender."

Aunt Eunice was busy telling me I put the vegetables in too soon, they were going to turn to mush before the meat was half-done. Then she said she only has stew in summer if she's got to have the fire going for washing or canning or baking bread.

That's when Mama walked in and said, "Nobody gets through life without making a few mistakes," and Aunt Eunice sniffed and said, "It does seem Abigail makes more than her fair share."

The stew did get done finally. The meat was still a little tough. Joel chewed away. He rolled his eyes and said, "No sacrifice is too great if it makes Abby into a good cook."

Later Aunt Eunice sent over a raisin pie (it was really good), so then of course he had to say, "Aunt Eunice just didn't want to see her favorite nephew starve to death."

Friday, July 22

Last night I dreamed I wrote a cookbook.

Maybe I will if I ever learn to cook. If I do, I'll be sure to put in the exact measurements, and there won't be any "cook until fork tender" in it. That's too much like guessing. If the dish turns out all right, it's a downright miracle.

This afternoon Aunt Eunice made a special trip over here to tell Mama she heard that the Pritchetts were thinking of hiring a girl to help old Mrs. Pritchett. I listened in *absolute horror* because I could guess who Aunt Eunice had in mind. Me. I was right, too.

"It would be a real good opportunity for Abigail," said Aunt Eunice. "She'd learn a lot. Mrs. Pritchett is a good housekeeper and an *excellent* cook."

"But the Pritchetts' farm . . . " I burst out, "it's way out in the middle of nowhere!"

"It is not. You do exaggerate, Abigail," Aunt Eunice said. "It would be splendid experience." I really held my breath and looked at Mama with my most forlorn expression.

" . . . And you needn't put that hound dog look on your face, child. Plenty of girls your age and younger go out to work."

Mama was hemming a skirt. She snipped off her thread and said, "I wouldn't think of sending Abby out to work even if she were old enough, which she isn't. She hasn't even finished school."

"I was only trying to help."

"I know," said Mama. "It's not necessary, Eunice."

"The Malone girls were both out working at twelve."

"But not Abby," said Mama firmly. I breathed a great sigh of relief and felt like saying "so there!" to Aunt Eunice, but didn't. I don't mind taking care of the little Smith Kenyons once in a while. I don't mind *much* that is, but they only live down the street.

Mama said later that Aunt Eunice had to go out to work young herself and secretly regrets not finishing school.

I don't know how Mama can always find a reason for

the way people act however peculiar it is. She thinks most people would behave properly if only they had been brought up right . . . or weren't sick in the head.

Aunt Eunice, on the other hand, says some people were just plain born ornery. I hate to admit it, but sometimes I agree with Aunt Eunice.

After Aunt Eunice left and Mama went upstairs to rest, Joel came in, and I could tell right away something was wrong.

"Where's Mama?" he asked.

"Upstairs."

He stopped with his hand on the banister and asked, "Is she sick again?"

"Just resting," I said. "And she said for no one to bother her unless somebody broke a leg or the roof fell in," so he cut off about half a loaf of bread and went out back, where Luke Trabert was waiting.

The wind ruffled up his hair and he pulled on his cap. Joel is changing. His face has gotten older somehow and thinner, but his shoulders are broadening out. His jaw is beginning to jut out so it doesn't quite seem to fit his face anymore. His nose, too.

Something is bothering him. He still hasn't told Mama he wants to quit school. Maybe that's it.

CHAPTER 7

❧❧❧❧❧

Monday, July 25

It's hot, and the air feels heavy. There's been heat lightning off to the west, but not a drop of rain. I wish it would rain. Then maybe it would cool off.

Mama has decided that one day a week I am to have full charge of supper—the planning, shopping, and cooking, also the cleaning up after.

Joel said he didn't know whether his stomach could live through it, but Mama told him to shush up. Then she hunted through the dining room sideboard until she found her recipe box, the little brown wooden one her father made for her. With her name carved in the lid. I've wanted it for my own for just years and years. I thought sure if she gave it to anybody it would be Damaris. But she didn't. It has all her own recipes in it.

I told her I didn't really need it seeing as I have *Mrs. Brown's Receipt Book.* She said Mrs. Brown was all very well, but her own recipes were tried and true and also much simpler.

"I hope I don't waste too much food," I said doubtfully, and she smiled and gave me a quick hug.

"You aren't to worry about that," she said, but I do anyway. I'll probably dream about Aunt Eunice checking the garbage can.

Damaris found out this evening what is bothering Joel. It's what I thought. He hasn't figured out how to tell Mama he wants to quit school. Damaris told him, "Don't even ask," and that really started something.

"Why not?" Joel said.

"Mama won't ever agree, and besides you have to think of your future."

"Luke quit school, and he's doing all right."

"Luke Trabert has to support his mother. You don't—"

"What am I supposed to do? Sit back and let you and Mama support me?" Joel said, stomping out.

Damaris sighed as the door banged shut after him and said, "It would just about kill Mama if he quit school."

"I expect he knows that. If only Papa . . . " If only Papa would send us some money is what I started to say.

"Papa helps when he can," Damaris said, which is exactly what Mama always says, so I guess it's true.

Tuesday, July 26

The wind is hot and dry, and the garden is parched. Uncle George says he is afraid when the rains do come it will be too late to save the crops. Hard times for farmers mean hard times for him, too. They can't buy hardware. They can't pay for it, anyway.

I wish it would cool off. Maybe Mama would feel better. I think all this sewing she does is tiring her out, but she says it's the heat and the wind that's making her feel as parched as the corn and wheat fields look.

Mrs. Smith Kenyon asked Mama to make six shirts for her husband. When Mama hesitated, Mrs. Smith Kenyon said there was no rush for the shirts but she hoped the kids' clothes would be done for their trip to see her folks.

Mama said she would do her best. That means she will sew half the night to get it all done.

Wednesday, July 27

Aunt Eunice wanted Mama to go to the Ladies' Aid meeting with her this afternoon. Mama said she couldn't because she had to finish this sewing for Mrs. Smith Kenyon.

"She's leaving *again?*" Aunt Eunice said, screwing up her mouth as though she'd bit into a green persimmon. "My land, that woman spends a lot of time traveling." She stopped for breath, and then she said, "But surely, Emily, you can spare a little time for the Ladies' Aid."

"You better go on without me," Mama said.

"Are you ailing again, Emily?"

"Just tired. I expect it's this weather."

Aunt Eunice said, "I know why, and it's not the weather. You've been working too hard. Even a horse deserves a rest."

When Aunt Eunice talks like that, it makes me feel bad. I wish Mama didn't have to work so hard. I went over and leaned against her, and she put her arm around me.

"My goodness, Eunice," Mama said, "don't you go worrying Abby. She does take things to heart so. . . . "

"Well, somebody, naming no names, ought to be taking your welfare to heart, Emily," Aunt Eunice said, and I knew she was mostly talking about Papa. Then as she got up to go she turned to me and said, "You help your ma, Abigail," as if I wouldn't without her ever telling me.

"You and the kids come over for supper tonight, Emily. It won't be fancy, but it will be filling."

Mama said that was kind of her to ask, but she thought

she'd just have a little milk toast and go to bed early.

"Well, then I guess I'll be going. You do know how to fix milk toast for your mama, don't you, Abby?" Aunt Eunice had one hand on the doorknob, but I thought she never ever was going to leave.

"Yes, ma'am," I said. I certainly ought to, seeing as how it is just hot milk poured over buttered toast.

"Why doesn't Papa write?" I asked as Aunt Eunice finally went down the walk.

"He will," said Mama. She sounded tired as she put down her sewing. Then she went over to the mantel and picked up Papa's picture.

"Your papa is a fine-looking man," she said. "And he has handsome children." Her voice was choked as if she were going to cry, so I said I didn't think I wanted to be called "handsome" as that always makes me think of a horse. She laughed at that. I thought she would, which is why I said it.

Wednesday, August 3

A letter has come from Papa!

He says the geologic survey job didn't work out, and he expects to be taking a new job soon with the Travers Cotton Mill in Oakland, California, which is across the bay from San Francisco.

That means he'll be settled in a proper place. There

are schools in Oakland, so Mama says as soon as he saves enough for the tickets, he will probably send for us. I think she has been afraid something had happened and we would never hear from him again. I know I was.

There she was happy as could be, and I had to go and say, "I don't know whether I want to go out there to California at all."

"Of course you do, Abby," she said, half scolding and half laughing. "You'll like it just fine once you get used to it. It will be easier for all of us. And there won't be any of this nonsense about Joel leaving school to go to work. Your father will see to that."

Monday, August 8

We had some rain and a thunderstorm, but most of the storm seemed to go to the north.

Mama stayed up late working on Mrs. Raymond's dress. It wore her out. She said today she is just going to have to take herself in hand and quit babying herself so she'll be ready when Papa sends for us. Damaris and Joel both looked worried when she said that, though they tried not to let on.

I asked Damaris later what was wrong. She didn't answer for a minute. Then she said, "I don't know where Mama got the notion that Papa is going to send for us. Of course he'll send for us when he can, but maybe not right away. I hate for her to be disappointed."

"Maybe he doesn't want us," I said. Leave it to me to say the *wrongest* thing possible.

"Of course he wants us!" She glared at me. "What kind of a person doesn't want his family? You make Papa out like some kind of a monster, Abby."

"I didn't mean to." I should have remembered that Damaris can't stand for anybody to think Papa is anything less than *absolutely perfect.*

"Don't you ever say anything like that to Mama!"

"I won't," I promised, and I won't, but I can't help what I think, can I?

Sunday, August 14

Today was a lovely day. Mama says she is feeling better. Aunt Eunice brought over cold sliced ham and potato salad and greens from Uncle George's garden, and we had a picnic supper out on the screened porch. I made peach pie for dessert, and it turned out *absolutely perfect.* Even Aunt Eunice said so.

Afterward Mama played a tune on the piano! Only one, but it's the first time she played for a long time.

Wednesday, August 17

Another letter has come from Papa. He says he doesn't

think the boardinghouse where he is living is the proper place for a family. He is looking around for a house we can afford, but he doesn't know if he can find one much before the new year.

He says he is very busy getting started at the Travers Cotton Mill. The owner is a widow lady who needs all the help she can get. He did send some money. He said he was sorry to hear Mama was under the weather and hoped she'd be better soon.

Mama said, "Well, what's a few months more? It will just give us more time to get ready."

Joel says he is going to talk to Mama about taking the job at the telegraph office. He says he might as well if we are going to be here until New Year's.

Friday, August 19

When Mama got up from the sewing machine yesterday morning, she went all faint and would have fallen except for Joel. Luckily he was still home and caught her.

I ran for Dr. Raymond as fast as I could go. He told Mama to stay in bed and take it easy. We could have told her that ourselves, though she probably wouldn't pay attention to us.

I have been doing the cooking since Mama has been under the weather. Joel says it's not bad, considering. In fact he said my biscuits are "quite superior"!

Tuesday, August 23

Mama has been most awfully sick. Aunt Eunice says Dr. Raymond can't be beat for fixing broken bones, but I don't think he knows what to do for Mama. He just tells her to stay in bed and take that nasty tonic, which doesn't seem to be doing much good.

Thursday, August 25

Maybe the tonic did do some good. She does seem some better and has been up sitting in a chair in her room. She took a little chicken soup today and said it did her a world of good. Aunt Eunice told me how to make it, and it turned out really good. Even Joel liked it. And after Mama had the soup, she said she'd be on her feet in no time, what with all the good care we've been giving her.

Friday, August 26

Since she's been feeling better, Joel went up to talk to Mama about the job at the telegraph office. He wasn't gone long.

"What did she say?" I said when he came down. And when he didn't answer right off I said, "I bet she said, 'No, absolutely not,' as usual."

"She said all right."

"All right! She didn't fuss about school?"

"No," he said, not looking me straight on.

"That's not like Mama," I said.

"No, it isn't."

"I wonder what changed her mind."

"She said I'm old enough to make my own decisions."

That should have made Joel happy, but I don't think it did. The wind's come up, and I can hear the Kansas Pacific locomotive hooting away out there in the night. It's a lonesome old sound.

It's mighty queer, Mama changing her mind like that. I wish I could keep from worrying. I try not to. I keep trying to think of something else, but it's real hard with this big old knot twisting up inside.

Wednesday, August 31

Aunt Eunice says she will come and sit with Mama while I go to school. I said I could stay home, but Aunt Eunice said that would just worry Mama more.

Joel didn't get the job at the telegraph office after all. They hired an older man with a family, so he's still going to school and working here and there part-time where he can, mostly down at the railroad station.

Monday, September 12

Uncle George sent over one of the Malone girls to help

with the wash. Mama got really upset at that. She said he shouldn't, that he can't afford the extra expense. She keeps telling us we must watch out for each other and not be a burden.

The least little thing upsets her. It's just awful to see her cry. We don't know what to do. Dr. Raymond gave her a powder to calm her down. He told Uncle George to wire Papa. Mama overheard and got so upset that Uncle George had to promise not to.

Monday, September 26

Aunt Eunice couldn't come today, so I stayed home from school. I can't keep my mind on my books at all these days.

Mama didn't say anything about my staying home. She slept all day and didn't eat a thing or even ask for water.

Tuesday, September 27

Dr. Raymond came again today, and Pastor Needham, too. Dr. Raymond told Uncle George he'd best send Papa a telegram. I don't think Mama heard.

Wednesday, September 28

Everybody keeps talking to each other: Dr. Raymond to Uncle George to Aunt Eunice. They stop when I come in the room, but I heard Dr. Raymond say something about Mama having a "rheumatic heart," whatever that is. He asked Uncle George if she'd had scarlet fever as a child.

Friday, September 30

Dr. Raymond is a QUACK!

I don't care if he is Dolly's pa. He says Mama . . . won't . . . can't get better . . . but he's wrong. Wrong, wrong, wrong!

CHAPTER 8

October

Dr. Raymond wasn't wrong. I was.

They've burned sulfur in Mama's room, and Aunt Eunice has sold our piano to Mr. Buttchenbacher. Nothing is the way it ought to be anymore.

I can't write about Mama dying. Not now. Maybe someday. Even when I'm all cried out on the outside, I still feel like crying on the inside.

This is an awful, dreary, wet, dismal, mournful old

month. I hate it! Aunt Eunice says it will pass. Uncle George pats me on the shoulder. He feels like crying, too. I can tell by his eyes. I don't think I will ever like October again.

Damaris sent Papa a telegram. When he answered he didn't say anything about coming to Estes himself. He said Uncle George was to make all the "arrangements."

I guess that was sensible. Aunt Eunice says it was. She said Papa couldn't have gotten here in time to do anything useful. He didn't say anything about Damaris, or Joel and me, either, or what we ought to do. It seems like he should have done that, doesn't it?

Aunt Eunice says we can't live by ourselves in our house. She says it isn't suitable even if we could afford the rent and that we must move in with her and Uncle George until we hear more from Papa.

Aunt Eunice found an old diary when she was going through Mama's things and said I might as well have it. It belonged to Mama when she was a girl. I like having something of Mama's. I keep it under my pillow at night. It makes her feel closer.

Saturday, October 8

Today Aunt Eunice told Mrs. Smith Kenyon, "It's our plain duty to take in those poor orphaned children."

I hate being "a plain duty," though it's not so bad being Uncle George's "plain duty" as it is being Aunt

Eunice's. We aren't "orphaned children" anyway, not whole orphans since we still have Papa.

Monday, October 10

Joel and I went back to school today, and Damaris went to work. Joel looks as pale as if he'd been sick, and Damaris has great dark circles under her eyes.

Mr. Buttchenbacher sent for the piano. I hate for him to have it! It should be Damaris's. She plays almost as well as Mama does . . . did. Aunt Eunice says not to fuss, that it was kind of him to take it off our hands and we can use the money.

Tuesday, October 11

They sold the rest of Mama's things, except for the cots Uncle George brought over and set up in the attic. That's where Damaris and I sleep.

Joel sleeps downstairs in the boys' room. He has a shakedown on the floor. The four little boys sleep in two double beds. Joel tried sleeping with Clay and Dennis the way Aunt Eunice told him to, but they near kicked him out of bed. I guess there would be more room in with the littlest ones, Delbert and Stewart, but they aren't housebroken yet.

Aunt Eunice doesn't like the windows open at night. She says night air is unhealthy, but Mama says . . . used to say . . . fresh air was good for us day or night. Damaris and I open our attic window a little bit anyway, but Joel's can't be opened at all. It's stuck shut with old paint.

Joel says the floor is okay and come spring he'll sleep outside. If we're still here in the spring, that is.

Sunday, October 16

It's been cold and raining some. Today it was just gray and gloomy all day. I have been having bad dreams.

Damaris's employer, Mr. Buttchenbacher, brought her home from church in his buggy. I don't believe she wanted to ride with him but she didn't know how to say no.

He is awfully old. He must be as old as Papa, and he has funny teeth, regular old horse teeth. He has a big house way out on the edge of town. Aunt Eunice says he is looking for a wife and she expects Damaris could set her cap for him and that would fix us up fine, as there is plenty of room in that "mansion" for us all.

Damaris got all pink and said she wasn't planning on marrying anyone, especially Mr. Karl Buttchenbacher. Then she got her coat, and we walked out to the cemetery.

I know Mama's gone to heaven, but she seems closer when we go out there . . . as though that was the door she went through. Aunt Eunice says time heals all wounds and that I'll get over pining away, but I don't know. Lots of times I feel like everything I eat gets stuck halfway down between my mouth and my stomach.

Monday, October 17

I'm feeling mixed up about Aunt Eunice.

I was doing up the dishes and looking out the window at the big old cottonwood out back. The wind came up and the leaves swirled down. It made me feel so bad that Mama's not here to see them.

"Abby?" Aunt Eunice came up behind me and put her arms around me. "It's your mama you're thinking about, isn't it?"

"Yes, ma'am," I said, and rubbed my eyes with my wet, soapy hand, which didn't help any. "I keep thinking if only I'd helped her more . . . if I'd known how, maybe she'd still be here. . . . "

"Listen, Abby," she said, "there wasn't anything you could do. You did the best you could for her. It wasn't your fault your mama died, and don't you ever think so."

"How did you know what I was thinking?" I asked.

"Because that's how I felt when my mama died. I was just your age."

It surely is hard to think of Aunt Eunice being my age. Sometimes she doesn't seem so bad. I told her about my dreams, how I dream of Mama being dead. She patted me on the shoulder and said the dreams would go in time.

Everyone has been kind to us, even Dolly's ma. She sent over a three-layer Lady Baltimore cake, which none of us could eat a bite of. Today I went to Dolly's after school, and Mrs. Raymond asked, "How are things going, Abigail?"

"All right," I said. Sometimes you don't know how to answer a question, but I'm not sure Mrs. Raymond expected one for she went right on saying how good it was of Uncle George and Aunt Eunice to take us in with "their financial situation being what it is."

I was still puzzling over that before supper when Aunt Eunice asked me to go out and keep an eye on Delbert and little Stewie, who were out in the backyard trying to stuff the Smith Kenyons' cat into their old go-cart. I took my sketchbook and charcoal with me but had to set them down while I rescued Caesar.

I had just sat down myself when Joel came home. I told him what Dolly's ma said about Uncle George's "financial situation" and asked him what he supposed she meant.

"Folks need hardware," he said, "but they can't pay for it, and then Uncle George can't pay what he owes to the bank for his stock, that's the stuff on the shelves. There's the rent to pay every month, too."

"But, Joel," I said, rescuing my drawing pad from Stewart, who was chewing on a corner, "you and Damaris help out."

"As much as we can." I didn't find out what else he

was going to say because right then we looked down and saw Stewart. He grinned toothless and cheerful with charcoal smeared from ear to ear and down the front of his coverall, and we both halfway laughed.

"Doesn't seem right to laugh . . . with Mama gone," I said doubtfully, as I rescued my drawing pad and charcoal and began to scrub at Stewart's face with my handkerchief.

"I think it's all right, Abby. Mama wouldn't want us to be sad for always," Joel said, "not on her account."

I guess he's probably right, but it made me feel bad all over again to think I could laugh with Mama gone.

CHAPTER 9

꙳꙳꙳꙳꙳

Tuesday, October 18

Letters came from Papa today. His writing is so full of curlicues it's hard to read.

He said we must "remain in the tender care of your aunt and uncle in this hour of tragic loss," and that we should be "obedient to them and diligent in both work and study," until he sends for us.

He told Uncle George he was still living at a boardinghouse "unsuitable for young children" and that in the past he had suffered certain financial reverses but that his new job at the Travers Cotton Mill is going well and he hopes to be able to send for us when he is properly situated.

"Properly situated!" Aunt Eunice sniffed. "That means when he figures out what to do with them! I don't suppose he thought to send any money, did he?"

"Now, Eunice," Uncle George said, "I expect John is having a hard time of it."

"And I expect we're living in the lap of luxury and dining on caviar and hummingbird tongues ourselves." That must have been a joke (though it's kind of hard to tell with Aunt Eunice). Except on Sundays or when the preacher comes, we eat a lot of mush for supper. It does taste good, though, with plenty of Daisy's butter and cream on it.

"Everything will work out," Uncle George said.

"I'd like to know how," she said, and then they went into their room and shut the door.

It makes me feel uncomfortable. I guess it would be best for us to go out to Papa. If he ever sends for us. If he ever wants to send for us. I expect Damaris wouldn't like for me to say that.

Wednesday, October 19

It's beginning to get very cold up here in the attic. I need new shoes. Mine pinch my toes and are almost worn through the soles.

Sunday, October 23

Mr. Buttchenbacher brought Damaris and me home from church today when it started to snow. He sat awfully close to her. She kept trying to scoot over toward the edge and still be polite and not fall off.

Monday, October 24

At supper Aunt Eunice said she'd seen Mr. Buttchen-bacher when she was pricing shoes for the kids. He told her he would give her a good deal if she told Damaris to be real nice and polite to him. Aunt Eunice said he made it sound like a joke, but she could tell he really meant it.

"Just how nice did you want her to be, Eunice?" Uncle George said, and Aunt Eunice looked all flustered.

"You know very well what I mean," she said.

"Don't rush the girl," Uncle George said. "We don't have to marry her off to get along, not so long as the cornmeal holds out and Daisy don't go dry."

"It won't hurt Damaris to be polite to the man."

"I'm always polite," Damaris said.

"Also stubborn," Joel whispered to me as he passed the cornmeal mush and the milk. Damaris *is* stubborn, though most people probably don't notice because she's so pretty. I used to be jealous of Damaris. I'm over it now, mostly over it, anyway.

Wednesday, November 2

I saw Mrs. Smith Kenyon when I went to the store for coal oil. She wants me to watch her children after school two afternoons a week so she can have time for her painting. All six of them! The oldest, Junior Smith Kenyon, who is eight, will be the worst. He collects toads, frogs, and bugs.

Aunt Eunice said that Mrs. Smith Kenyon's painting is a lot of foolishness, but if she wants to throw her money away I might as well be the one to take advantage of it. I am to start next week.

CHAPTER 10

※※※※※

November

Both my shoes are worn through now.

Aunt Eunice says it's a pity I can't wear a pair Damaris has outgrown that still have some good left in them, but my feet have gotten too big. Sure enough. I hadn't noticed, but my feet are bigger than Damaris's and Aunt Eunice's, too, though I'm not as tall as either one of them. She said it in front of Dolly, and it was very embarrassing!

This morning Damaris saw me putting a new cardboard in my shoe to cover the hole. She went to her purse, took out a dollar and told me to go down to the Emporium after school and get a new pair.

"The cardboard works all right," I said. I know she doesn't have much left from her salary after giving money to Aunt Eunice, and she's been saving for a new coat. That old one of Mama's she's wearing doesn't look very nice. Dolly keeps telling me it's important to look your best when you go out to business.

"Do it," Damaris said. "Money won't be much good if you come down with pneumonia."

Damaris seems to figure it's her job to take care of us in Mama's place now—as though I didn't have sense enough to take care of my own self. She treats Joel the same way, especially when he talks about quitting school—which he still does—but he ignores her. I can't.

I didn't argue with her about the shoes, though, because it's getting cold and that cardboard is mighty thin. All I said was, "Shall I ask about that special price Mr. Buttchenbacher offered Aunt Eunice?"

"Pay the full price," she said. "We don't want to be beholden to Mr. Buttchenbacher."

I was glad. I don't want to have to be grateful to Mr. Buttchenbacher. It's bad enough with Aunt Eunice and Uncle George and they're relatives.

Mama always told us we should be independent and

take care of our own selves so we wouldn't be under obligation to anyone.

After school I walked down to the Emporium to look for my shoes. Who should be there already but Dolly and her ma. They were there to pick out some black kid party slippers for Dolly, but Mrs. Raymond wasn't in any great big hurry. She kept finding fault with the slippers, though they all looked nice to me and I was wishing I could have a pair. In fact, I was pea green with envy.

Aunt Eunice would probably tell me that was another flaw in my character. Sometimes I know exactly what Aunt Eunice is going to say before she opens her mouth.

While Mrs. Raymond had that poor clerk running back and forth with shoes, she kept looking toward the office where Mr. Buttchenbacher was working. They have electric lights in the Emporium, though most everybody else in town still uses gas or oil lamps. You could see the electric light shining on that bald spot on the back of his head.

Maybe he felt Mrs. Raymond's eyes boring into him because pretty soon he rubbed the back of his head and neck and came out of his office.

Mrs. Raymond bounced up and rushed over to him, leaving the poor clerk waving the last pair of slippers to empty air.

"Karl Buttchenbacher, you're just the man I want to

see," she said. She sounded as young and giggly as Dolly, not a bit the way she does when she talks to me or Dolly or Aunt Eunice even.

Mrs. Raymond certainly is a good talker. She talked Mr. Buttchenbacher into having a Thanksgiving Benefit Tea at his house to raise money for the Estes Memorial Library Fund.

"It's your civic duty, Karl," she said, "you being our *leading citizen*. . . . " Her voice went all creamy, and there Mr. Buttchenbacher was lapping it up, practically licking his whiskers.

" . . . Think what it will mean to the town," Mrs. Raymond went on. I was certainly surprised when Mr. Buttchenbacher agreed!

"I thought he'd say no for sure," I whispered to Dolly.

"Nobody says no to Mama," Dolly said.

After I paid for my own plain old button-top school shoes, I went home and told Aunt Eunice. She said Mrs. Raymond "could talk anybody into anything" and that the Tea ought to raise a good deal of money as she wasn't the only one in town dying for a look inside Mr. Buttchenbacher's mansion. I am getting tired of writing Mr. Buttchenbacher so I think I will just call him Mr. B.

Mrs. Smith Kenyon told Aunt Eunice it showed Mrs. Raymond must be a good soul at heart to put her talents to work in such a good cause as the Estes Memorial Library. Aunt Eunice said yes, but she didn't sound as if she meant it.

I told Joel later I didn't think I personally would have said Dolly's ma is a good soul at heart. He laughed at me and said, "You better watch out. You're beginning to sound like Aunt Eunice—"

"Joel Edwards!" I said, positively *enraged*. "What an awful thing to say!"

"Just teasing, Abby," he said.

Sunday, November 20

Unfortunately for Aunt Eunice, Clay and Delbert broke out in measles and Stewart started cutting molars so she couldn't go to Mr. Buttchenbacher's. Uncle George said wild horses couldn't drag him to a benefit tea if you paid him in gold bullion, so Aunt Eunice said it was up to Damaris and me to go and do the honors for the family since we have already had the measles.

It was just almost more than a body could bear, she said, not to see the inside of that house. She'd watched them cart in mahogany for the woodwork and marble for the fireplaces, and here she was missing her one big opportunity. We were to be sure to keep our eyes peeled so we could tell her everything.

So there Damaris and I were climbing up the stairs to Mr. Buttchenbacher's "mansion." It's way out almost by itself on the edge of town, a kind of lonesome location with nothing much but fields and sky between it and the Rocky Mountains. It didn't seem lonesome this afternoon, though, with all those people, mostly ladies, taking the opportunity to satisfy their curiosity.

Mr. Buttchenbacher saw us come in and came right over to talk to Damaris. I spotted Dolly and the food. Two Irish girls were serving. One was Bridget, who works three days a week for the Raymonds. The other was her sister Mary. They were carrying around silver trays full of tarts and cookies and those little frosted cakes Mrs. Raymond calls petits fours. Since nobody seemed to be counting, Dolly and I stuffed ourselves until we couldn't hold a crumb more, and then we started looking around.

It certainly is a big house. There were two high-ceilinged parlors paneled in dark mahogany with marble fireplaces in each. The curtains were heavy lace, the drapes dark red velvet fringed with balls, and the carpet felt two inches thick.

"Turkish," Dolly whispered. Then when nobody was looking we sneaked upstairs.

There was nothing much to see up there but bedrooms. The beds had great tall carved headboards, and the chests were marble topped. At the end of the hall was a child's room with a wooden rocking horse.

"But he doesn't have any children," I whispered.

"He did," Dolly said. "A little boy who died and is buried out in the Estes cemetery. My mama told me."

All of a sudden I had this most awful feeling that all those tarts and petits fours were going to come right back up. How could I giggle and have a good time with Dolly?

How could I forget for a minute that Mama was out there in the cemetery all by herself alone?

I went and found Damaris and told her I felt sick and was going to walk home. She said she would go with me, but Mr. Buttchenbacher wouldn't let us walk. He drove us back himself.

Monday, November 21

Everyone said how lucky it was we had nice weather for the Tea. Now it's raining cats and dogs, and I had to tell Uncle George there's a leak in the roof. Water's dripping into the attic, though fortunately not on our beds.

After dinner as Aunt Eunice got pans out to put under all the leaks, she said she'd heard from more than one party that Mr. B. had paid a considerable lot of attention to Damaris. Then she began to go on about how Damaris can be Mrs. Buttchenbacher if she plays her cards right.

Joel whispered to me, "Damaris Buttchenbacher. How does that sound to you, Abby?"

I giggled and said, "Purely awful!"

Aunt Eunice fixed her eye on me, said it wasn't a matter for levity, and sent me up to put the pans under the leaks.

"I don't think Mama would like Aunt Eunice talking like that," I told Damaris when she came up to bed. Her hair was all gold and brown in the lamplight, and the little tendrils curled around her face as she combed it out.

"Mama tried to think what was best for us all," Damaris said, and then she blew out the lamp. I stayed awake a long time listening to the rain and hearing the *plink plunk* of the drip in the pan. What would Mama think was best for us all? I heard Damaris turn over and knew she couldn't sleep either.

"I wish Mama were here," I said.

"I do, too, Abby," she said. Then she told me to go to sleep, and I finally did but I had bad dreams.

Thursday, December 8

Uncle George has caught a terrible cold. Aunt Eunice made him soak his feet in hot water and put a mustard plaster on his chest front and back and rubbed him with warm turpentine and oil.

It seems like that ought to do the trick. We all have colds, and it sounds, Uncle George says, like a lungers' convention, which upset Aunt Eunice.

"Don't even joke like that," she said. A lunger is somebody who has tuberculosis.

Wednesday, December 28

Christmas wasn't much fun. Aunt Eunice doesn't hold

with big celebrations. After all, she says, the most important thing is that it's the Lord's birthday.

Mama always said that, too, but she always had some little treat for us. Aunt Eunice gave us all wool socks, which is all right I guess. We needed them, but it wasn't much fun.

Mr. You Know Who is still bringing Damaris home from church. Aunt Eunice told Mrs. Smith Kenyon that she thought we might be hearing wedding bells in the spring. Joel said Aunt Eunice was cuckoo and had bats in her belfry. (He didn't say it where she could hear him, though.)

When Mrs. Smith Kenyon said Mr. B. seemed a little old for Damaris, Aunt Eunice said he was "a fine figure of a man all the same." Then she said, "Damaris was always very attached to her father. I don't think any mere boy could measure up to him in her mind."

"What about Luke Trabert? Isn't he interested in her?" asked Mrs. Smith Kenyon.

"Too young," said Aunt Eunice, as though that was a disease. "You know the old saying, 'better to be an old man's darling than a young man's slave.' "

"There's some truth in that, still"—Mrs. Smith Kenyon looked down at Myrna whose nose was running— "I don't think I'd want that for my Myrna." It's sort of difficult to imagine Myrna ever getting married to anyone.

The Smith Kenyons are going to be moving. They are getting a house over on the other side of town, out near Mr. Buttchenbacher's.

We didn't hear from Papa at all.

Sunday, January 1

It's a new year. 1905. I wonder what will happen this year.

Joel wants to go out West. I'd *hate* for him to go away. He talks about leaving when he is sixteen, which won't be long, and says maybe he and Luke will join the army. Then he says he's teasing, that he'll go to work when he's finished eighth grade and make enough to take care of us all.

Damaris used to talk about studying music. She never does now. I wonder if she's forgotten or if it's because there is no money or if she thinks school is more important for Joel.

Joel knows a lot already. He tells me more than I want to know about a lot of things. Damaris says he *must* go on to high school and the university so he can become an engineer or maybe a geologist, since he's interested in rocks and such as well as engines.

Aunt Eunice says there isn't enough money for such "highfalutin" ideas, not unless our papa can manage it, which she says "is about as likely as Daisy hatching ducks" and "that will be the day."

Uncle George had to take off another couple of days from work. He still has a cough, though the rest of us are over ours.

This afternoon Dolly and I walked over to the other side of town to see where the Smith Kenyons' new house is. It's not new exactly but new to them and bigger than their old house. Junior won't have to sleep in the parlor, and Myrna will have a room to herself.

Dolly has always had a room to herself, being an only child, but she says it's lonely. After we looked at the Smith Kenyons' house, we went back to Dolly's to have some of her ma's tarts made with raspberry preserves, which are luscious and positively melt in your mouth.

The only trouble was we had to listen to Mrs. Raymond while we ate. She asked me if we'd heard from Papa over the holidays, and I had to say no. I know she thought it was peculiar.

Then Mrs. Raymond told Dolly to show me the gold locket her papa gave her for Christmas. It's heart shaped and it opens up so Dolly can put pictures inside.

About then I began to feel sick to my stomach and had to go home.

CHAPTER 11

❦❦❦❦❦

It's still January

It seems as though it has been January forever, even though the month has hardly begun. It's cold, cold enough Uncle George says to freeze his whiskers off.

I have become a Mother's Help. I am to stay at the Smith Kenyons' during the week now that they live on the other side of town and come home after lunch Saturday for the weekend.

I feel uncomfortable staying there at night, but Mrs. Smith Kenyon says she needs help mornings as well as after school and at night, too. She said I could sleep in with Myrna or else there's a partially finished room up in the attic and they would put a cot up there for me. I prefer the attic. Myrna talks in her sleep. She also kicks.

There was a great commotion today getting Mr. Smith Kenyon off. Since he works for the railroad, he's gone a lot. After he left, Mrs. Smith Kenyon got out her paints and began to do her china painting. She is very artistic, but she says she mostly works when Mr. Smith Kenyon is gone because the smell of her oils and turpentine makes his eyes burn.

She reads a lot at night. Mr. Smith Kenyon must not like what she reads because Myrna said, "Mama always puts her books away before Papa comes home."

Arthur Junior brought along his collection of bugs, frogs, snakes, and such when they moved. Fortunately they're all mounted or pickled and as dead as doornails at the moment, but I'm not looking forward to spring.

I told him Joel collected rocks when he was eight in hopes that Junior would change his interests. Myrna says it's hopeless, that Junior just likes things that slither and wiggle and fly.

Myrna is six but acts like a little old lady sometimes. She says she's glad I'm here because maybe now her mama won't need to keep her out of school so much to help tend the babies.

Brandon and Violetta are twins. They're four and have their own language that they talk to each other. The two youngest are boys, Kevin and Willis, and neither one of them is what you'd call housebroken, but Kevin, that limb of Satan, surely ought to be.

Wednesday, January 9

I get up at six o'clock (A.M. that is), light the fire, get the children up, see that they're dressed, and change the baby's diaper if necessary, which it always is. I empty the slop jars and put the bedrooms in order before school. There surely are a lot of beds and cribs to make up in this house. After school I wash up the breakfast and lunch dishes, help get dinner, wash dishes (again), and put the children to bed. Then I do my lessons.

Damaris bought me a nice bar of imported white castile soap made with pure olive oil, but Kevin dropped it in the sanitary convenience, which is what Mrs. Smith Kenyon calls the outhouse.

Joel has not been getting much work at all this month on account of the weather.

After my first week as a Mother's Help, I said, "Joel, I know how anxious you are to work, so I will make the supreme sacrifice. You can take my place at the Smith Kenyons'."

"No, thanks," he said. He's not so dumb.

"I don't know what you are complaining about, Abigail," Aunt Eunice said. (I wouldn't have said anything if I'd known she could hear me.) "It's splendid experience for you. You would just be frittering away your time otherwise. It will stand you in good stead when you get married."

I don't believe I will ever get married, so all this experience is not going to do me much good, is it?

Monday, January 14

This house doesn't look new anymore. It wasn't really new when the Smith Kenyons moved in, but it looked new. Now it looks about the way their old house did only they have more room to spread around in.

Mrs. Smith Kenyon has been rushing around all day with her hair all tied up in a dish towel. The first thing she said to me was, "We must really scurry around and set things to right, as Arthur (that's Mr. S. K.) will be home tonight, and dear Arthur is an extremely tidy man."

She bent down and collected a pair of dirty socks from under the sofa. Then she sat back and laughed and said, "I'm sure we are a great trial to him. Fortunately I do believe he loves us anyway."

There is certainly a lot of washing up to be done around here, but nothing ever seems really clean. Maybe it's because all these children dirty things up faster than we can clean them.

Mrs. Smith Kenyon says I will be a big help this summer when canning time comes around. Her specialty is sauerkraut. There's a big crock of it down in the cellar. She says we have to watch the kids. They're always sneaking down there to swipe some. You'd think they could find something else, wouldn't you?

The house did look pretty good when Mr. Smith Kenyon came home, though it's best he doesn't look under the beds.

"Out of sight, out of mind!" says Mrs. Smith Kenyon. Then she said, "Abby, when your husband comes home at night, always have the table set. Then he'll think supper's all but ready even if you've only just started."

I told that to Dolly and Mary Margaret Vincent. Mary Margaret said it sounded downright deceitful, but Dolly said it sounded right sensible to her. Mr. Smith Kenyon seems to be happy anyway. He may come home kind of tired and grumpy, but pretty soon Mrs. Smith Kenyon has him all smiling and cheerful, so I guess she must be doing something right.

Mary Margaret moved to town last summer. Her father is Professor Vincent, who teaches voice and elocution and piano. Mary Margaret has pale eyes and pale eyelashes and isn't really pretty but she doesn't seem to know it. Dolly says Professor Vincent just dotes on her even if she isn't. Dolly and Mary Margaret have gotten to be friends since I've had to be at the Smith Kenyons' every afternoon.

Saturday, January 24

We walked out to the cemetery today. It was cold and blowy, but it made us feel better. Joel kept getting ahead of us. His legs are so long now. Long and skinny. Not a speck of fat on him, Aunt Eunice says, as though it's a fault. Uncle George says he's just growing fast, that Papa is a fair-sized man and Joel will be, too.

"You're a fair-sized man yourself," Aunt Eunice said. "Joel favors the Hansens as much as he does the Edwardses."

Uncle George grinned at her and said, "That's not unnatural, Eunice, seeing that Emily was a Hansen." Emily is . . . was . . . our mama, and she was a Hansen before she married Papa and became an Edwards.

Damaris went back to the house ahead of us. After she'd gone, Joel stood there in his long, skinny bones and looked down at Mama's grave with the wooden cross. He'd pulled off his cap and his hair was all streaky gold.

"Someday," he said, looking down at the marker, "we'll get a proper stone for Mama."

It was still cold as we walked home, but somehow I felt better, warmer inside. Joel started telling me about the land, how once upon a time a couple billion years ago it was covered by a warm, shallow sea.

I couldn't believe that. Joel is always telling me things I can hardly believe. I started to say Pastor Needham didn't seem to think the whole earth had been around altogether a couple billion years, and Joel said, "Don't worry about it, Abby."

"But a couple billion years?" I said.

"The way I figure it is, God's time is different from preachers'." He looked way off to the west and said, "I figure Mama's in God's time." Then he put on his cap and said, "Come on, Abby, we better hurry or we'll miss supper."

When we got back, who was in the parlor talking politics to Uncle George but Mr. Buttchenbacher. He was waiting, he said, to take our beautiful sister to the pie social at the Methodist church.

Aunt Eunice said later it was a real surprise. She meant his going to the Methodist pie social, as he is a strong Lutheran. It wasn't as if he was going to services there though, she added. It was a surprise to me that Damaris was going with him.

Joel says Mr. B. must be going because the Methodist ladies bake good pies. That could be. Dolly's ma is a Methodist and hers are really scrumptious.

Mr. Buttchenbacher took out his gold watch and looked at it as I went upstairs. Damaris had just finished combing her hair.

"Your *friend* is waiting for you," I said.

"I know," she said, tucking up a stray wisp of hair.

"You don't have to make yourself beautiful for that old man!" I told her.

"I'm not," she said, "I'm just doing my hair."

"You've been so busy with your *friend*, I don't suppose you've written Papa again and asked him what we should do—"

"You suppose wrong." She pinned on her hat, an old one Aunt Eunice gave her. If Damaris wasn't so pretty, it would be ugly. It was ugly on Aunt Eunice.

"Did you tell him about Joel and school and—?"

"I told him everything."

"But he hasn't answered, has he?" I don't know what was the matter with me. It wasn't Damaris's fault Papa hasn't answered. It must have been Mr. Buttchenbacher sitting downstairs in the parlor big as life that made me so cross.

"Maybe he can't answer," she said slowly, a worried look in her eyes. Then she went downstairs, leaving me to stew in my own juice as Aunt Eunice says.

CHAPTER 12

❋❋❋❋❋

February

The schools have been closed because of snow, and the tracks from here to Kansas City are under five feet of snow.

Whatever did the Old Lady Who Lived in a Shoe do when it snowed? Maybe she had a Mother's Help.

I have found one way to keep the little Smith Kenyons busy. They are helping me write a story about a fairy child named Amaryllis who lives under the oak tree in summer and in the geranium pot in the winter. Even the twins who mostly live in their own world and just talk to each other have gotten interested in Amaryllis, and we have all been drawing pictures of her.

Mrs. Smith Kenyon has given me a copy of the *Magazine of the Arts* with some lovely drawings in it. I told her that when I copy pictures they turn out all right, but when I try to do what's in my own head it comes out all wrong or not what I want anyway. Mrs. Smith Kenyon said I must "practice, practice, practice" if I want to draw really well.

Wednesday, February 8

Today Junior Smith Kenyon found my diary. I caught him and Myrna trying to read it.

They had gotten to Damaris's name, and Myrna was sounding it out "*D, a, m,* Dam!" Her eyes got big as saucers, and she said, "That's a *swear* word!"

"It is not!" I said and snatched my diary back. Now I have to hide it. I put it under the loose board under the bed. I hope they don't find it there.

I don't write where anyone can see me if I can help it, much less let anyone read what I write. It would be like letting someone inside my head to see what I'm thinking.

Thursday, February 9

Mrs. Smith Kenyon showed me where she keeps the key to her bookcase so I can read if I want. She tries to keep it locked because that's where she keeps her art supplies as well as books, and she doesn't want the kids getting into her paint and turpentine.

Yesterday she forgot to lock it, and the baby, Willis, crawled over and got into the bookcase. I wasn't reading or drawing or anything, but I really need eyes in back of my head to keep track of all six kids.

I turned around, and there was Willis chewing on one of the books. Thank goodness he didn't poison himself on the turpentine. The book was one Dolly talks about. *What Every Young Woman Should Know.*

I took it away from him (had to give him a cookie to keep him from howling) and started to look through it, though some of the pages were a little soggy. Mrs. Smith Kenyon just laughed when I showed it to her and said "no harm done."

What Every Young Woman Should Know uses a whole lot of words to say it's a lot the same how cows, horses, and people get children.

Junior Smith Kenyon saw me reading *What Every Young Woman Should Know.* He has it all figured out. He told me, "Mother chickens and mother frogs have their babies in eggs outside their stomachs and people mothers have them on the inside."

This has been about the longest week I ever spent in my entire life. I can hardly wait until Saturday afternoon when I get to go home. Since becoming a Mother's Help I have positively decided I will never marry! Even if somebody asks me.

Saturday, February 11

This afternoon I told Joel I am not ever going to get married. He says I must, otherwise I will end up a withered old maid like Miss Lucas who teaches ancient history at the High School.

"Withered?" I said. "All dried up?"

"Like a prune," said Joel.

That's when I went to smack him, but he ducked.

"I absolutely positively am never going to get married! Even if I turn into a *raisin!*"

Why is it that Aunt Eunice always overhears me when I'd much rather she didn't? There she was right behind me, and I just knew from Joel's face that he knew it all the time.

"Never's a long time," she said. And then, "If you don't marry, what will you do, Abigail? You certainly have never been a brilliant scholar, so you can't expect to teach."

It is hard, I thought but did not say since Mama taught us to be polite to our elders, to be both a Mother's Help and a brilliant scholar.

I have, however, decided to become the best scholar I can if I can ever find time to study. I am really tired when all six little Smith Kenyons are finally corralled and put to bed.

Besides, Mr. Smith Kenyon wants all the lamps out by nine o'clock so as not to waste oil. I plan to buy candles with my own money. That way I won't have to use their oil when I study. Joel says I must be careful not to burn the house down. He needn't worry. By the time the little Smith Kenyons are through jumping around and asleep, I'll probably be too tired to open a book.

Tomorrow is Lincoln's Birthday.

Damaris and Joel had another argument over school. Joel said Mr. Lincoln never went to college, and Damaris said Joel isn't any Mr. Lincoln, and besides Mr. Lincoln never wanted to be an engineer.

Saturday evening

The minister from the Methodist church asked Damaris to sing in their choir. He said they would pay her, but Aunt Eunice says if she sings it should be at the Lutheran church.

Joel said something about becoming a Methodist because of their pies. I think he was making a joke, but Aunt Eunice got her feathers all ruffled up and told him he was endangering his immortal soul. I do wish she wouldn't say things like that.

Damaris looked from one to the other. Then she said she had decided not to sing for the Methodists after all. She told Joel and me later she didn't want to cause trouble, and that as long as we are living with Aunt Eunice and Uncle George we must go along with what they want. It seems to me we are mostly going along with what Aunt Eunice wants.

After supper I was in the parlor doing drawings for my story about Amaryllis when Luke Trabert came over and asked for Joel. I jumped up to call him. I am beginning to wonder if Dolly is right and he really comes in hopes of seeing Damaris. When I jumped up, I dropped my sketchbook smack dab on the floor, and Luke picked it up.

"These are quite good, Abby," he said, flipping through the pages. And I felt myself get all hot and flustered.

"It's sure no way to earn a living," said Aunt Eunice, who had come in the parlor with her sewing basket and a big pile of socks to darn.

"That's not all that counts," Luke said.

"Some people think drawing is a waste of time," I said, retrieving my sketchbook (and mentioning no names).

"Some people are right," said Aunt Eunice (whose name is the one I would have mentioned if I had not been not mentioning any).

"Not if you're Rembrandt or Rubens." Luke grinned at me.

"Both men," said Aunt Eunice. "That's some different. As Mr. Buttchenbacher says, all a girl needs to know is how to cook and sew and keep house. And darn socks, of course," she said, holding up one that was almost more hole than sock.

I dug my pencil so hard into the paper that I broke the point and spoiled the page. I do hate spoiling a page.

"You are careless, Abby," Aunt Eunice said as Joel came in. After he and Luke went off, Aunt Eunice looked at me sharply and said, "Whatever ails you, Abby?"

"Nothing," I said, keeping my eyes fixed on my paper.

"Are you sick? I hope you aren't bringing home some sickness from those Smith Kenyons."

"It just isn't fair," I burst out, not keeping my mouth shut as I guess I will never learn to do. "Why is it when people have money, what they say counts for more than what other people say?"

"It doesn't."

"What Mr. Buttchenbacher says does," I said.

"That's not so!" She bit her lip and then said slowly, "Of course that's not so. What a notion. What an odd child you are, Abby."

I expect she's right. Queer things do go on inside my head all right and my stomach, too. Once when I threw up on his best shiny boots, Papa said he never saw such a child for upchucking. At least I've outgrown that. I just feel sick inside sometimes.

Tuesday, February 14

Mrs. Smith Kenyon had a Valentine's Day party for her children. She showed me how to decorate the pink layer cake with squiggles of whipped cream, and the kids put red sugar bits on the cookies.

When we were walking home after school, Mary Margaret Vincent kept asking how many valentines Dolly and I got. We all got the same number at school, but Mary Margaret showed us two of the fancy lace ones she said were left at her door. She giggled and said they must be from secret admirers.

All she and Dolly talk about nowadays is boys—especially Luke Trabert and Joel! They have become better and better friends while I've been a Mother's Help. Dolly says we are still best friends, but how can she be best friends with Mary Margaret, too?

I wonder if Mary Margaret sent herself the valentines without names. That's probably terribly wicked of me to think, but I can't help it somehow. I try not to say anything mean, but I can't help what I think.

The sun started winking away on Mama's ring so the opals shone like fire. I expect Mama would tell me not to let Mary Margaret bother me.

Thursday, February 16

Sunday is Dolly's birthday. I bought three Irish linen

handkerchiefs for her with the money I earned at the Smith Kenyons'. I do like having money of my own.

This morning Mrs. Smith Kenyon told me to make hotcakes for the kids' breakfast. She said it would give her more time to paint. She does her painting on one end of the kitchen table and never clears it all the way off unless Mr. Smith Kenyon is home. It is a long table. We eat scrunched up at the one end.

"I'm not a very good cook," I said.

She just laughed. "My kids won't ever notice. And besides, syrup covers a lot of mistakes." Mrs. Smith Kenyon is certainly good tempered. She jiggles all over when she laughs, and she laughs a lot. When she paints, she works in a wrapper and doesn't wear corsets.

She says, "When your stomach is squished, so is your creativity." She also never uses a recipe when she cooks but just "improvises." She did tell me how to make the hotcakes, thank goodness. I don't think even the Smith Kenyons could eat what I would improvise on my own.

Actually they came out pretty good. Of course, to start with I had the pan too cold and then too hot and my first tries were all crooked, but they tasted all right, and the kids gobbled them up. I finally got the hang of it, and the last ones came out beautifully round.

Mrs. Smith Kenyon said they were very good (of course, she got some of the nice round ones) and that I would probably turn out to be a fine cook given time, which made me feel all plumped out and good.

Then she sighed and said, "Men are helpless in the kitchen. Most men that is. My hubby would just be helpless as a baby in the kitchen. Why, if I were taken, he'd probably be married again in no time at all. . . . "

I wasn't paying a whole lot of attention until she said, "Now your daddy, he's such a fine-looking man, so particular about his appearance. He's used to batching, I expect. No need for him to rush out and find a wife just because he doesn't know how to boil an egg, is there?"

She laughed and her chair creaked as she settled back into it. "My," she said, "I certainly am putting on weight. . . . " Then she said, "What *do* you hear from your daddy these days, Abby?"

I am always uncomfortable talking about Papa and didn't know what to say. Finally I said, "He's pretty busy I guess with his new job."

She kept asking questions, and pretty soon I was telling her he works at the Travers Cotton Mill in Oakland, and that, no, I didn't know exactly what he was doing there. I don't usually like to talk about Papa much because I know everybody in town must have thought it was peculiar when he didn't come when Mama was so sick.

Then Mrs. Smith Kenyon said, "Pity your daddy can't see his way clear to send for you children and see to your schooling. Mr. Avery Trabert, Luke's uncle, thinks a lot of your brother. He says he's very bright. And Damaris has a beautiful voice. Who knows what she could do with proper training. I hate to see talent wasted."

I do like Mrs. Smith Kenyon except when she starts asking about Papa in that roundabout way she did today.

Monday, February 20

Yesterday was Dolly's birthday party. Now that she's thirteen, she says her ma is going to get her a corset, and she's *happy* about it!

Since her birthday is so close to George Washington's her ma always makes a cherry pie for her party. There was a birthday cake with a cherry filling, too, and little cups of candies and nuts at each place and pink streamers from the chandelier.

Mary Margaret Vincent was there, too, of course. I try not to be jealous, but it's hard when they giggle and won't tell me why. Today Mary Margaret whispered something to Dolly and then said, "We musn't tell Abby. She's too young!"

They were probably talking about boys again, the way they usually do at school when we're eating lunch. Maybe not, though. It was right after that Mary Margaret said, "I hear Mr. Karl Buttchenbacher is courting your sister. I expect she'll be accepting him."

"I never heard anything so ridiculous in my whole entire life!" I said, giving her my most *scornful expression* and pretending it didn't bother me at all, but it did. I got to thinking maybe Papa ought to know, so today I went down and bought stationery and stamps to write him on my own. But now I can't decide what to say to him.

CHAPTER 13

❦❦❦❦❦

Friday, March 3

Well, I didn't die after all.

Yesterday Mrs. Smith Kenyon took Junior, Myrna, and the baby down to the Emporium to get new shoes. She left me home to tend the twins and Kevin. They were playing as nice as you please out on the back porch with their blocks and a wooden train set so I slipped upstairs to get my book from under the loose board. I hadn't had a chance to write in it for a couple of days.

The next thing I knew they were gone, all three of them, just plain gone.

I tell you I was some worried. I chased around looking for them "like a chicken with its head cut off" as Aunt Eunice says, all the time telling myself I never should have taken my eyes off them for a minute. I really was scared, thinking they'd gotten lost forever or drowned in a well or had broken their necks somehow and we'd find their poor little lifeless bodies in the creek.

They hadn't drowned or broken their necks. They were down in the cellar eating dried apples and sampling sauerkraut from Mrs. Smith Kenyon's crock.

I tried some myself before I herded them back up to the porch. It wasn't bad, not vinegary at all but crisp and tasty.

After supper I began to feel real poorly, and during the night I woke up thinking that sauerkraut sure must have gone bad. I thought I was dying and that my whole insides were about to fall out. I was certain for sure the next morning when I saw the blood.

Mrs. Smith Kenyon laughed and said I wasn't going to die and my insides weren't going to fall out, but I'd best go on home.

Aunt Eunice fussed and fumed and gave me *What Every Young Woman Should Know* to read.

I didn't get a chance to tell her I'd already mostly read

it because she kept talking and saying as how she wished my mama was here and that this was all according to Nature's Plan and how now that I was a young woman we must really start thinking about getting me fitted for corsets and putting up my hair.

I said I really didn't want to get fitted for a corset, and Aunt Eunice looked me up and down and said well she guessed I could get along with vests and union suits for a while longer as it didn't look as though I was ever going to have what you'd call a real well-developed figure.

I felt some relieved until she told me I was going to have to put up with this dried apple and sauerkraut business (which wasn't from dried apples and sauerkraut at all, but is part of Nature's Plan) every single month.

I really don't think much of Nature's Plan, especially since I don't plan to get married and won't be using Nature's Plan to become a mother. But it seems Nature doesn't ask you.

It turns out Dolly Raymond and Mary Margaret Vincent have already come up against Nature's Plan. Months ago. Wouldn't you know?

Sunday, March 12

Well, now I've really done it.

When I got back here this evening, Mrs. Smith Kenyon said she was glad to see me back because the children, especially Junior and Myrna, were driving her to distraction. Then she said, "Did you enjoy your weekend, Abby?"

I didn't know what to say, but nodded and mumbled, "Yes, ma'am." Which wasn't altogether the truth, but how could I tell Mrs. Smith Kenyon what happened?

Sunday was a purely awful day.

We went to church, of course, all of us, and then Aunt Eunice asked Pastor Needham and Mr. Buttchenbacher for Sunday dinner after services.

Mr. Buttchenbacher talked a lot about the Estes Emporium and how well it's doing in spite of what he called the general downturn in business.

He kept talking and talking and eating and eating Uncle George's food. In between he smiled with his big white horse teeth and kept looking at Damaris like she was strawberry ice cream, which she rather looked like in her new dress. She made it out of pink muslin with puffed sleeves and lace inserts.

Then finally he stopped looking at Damaris's front and asked Joel how he was doing in school.

Ordinarily Joel talks quite a lot. He can go on and on about the marvels of electricity and how someday we'll all be going around in horseless carriages and flying machines, but when it came to talking to Mr. Buttchenbacher, Joel turned into an *absolute clam.*

"A lad has to think of his future," Mr. B. said, taking out his gold toothpick. (Did I say he has a gold toothpick he keeps in his pocket along with his gold watch? Well, he does, and he uses it on those big white teeth.)

"Joel thinks a good deal about the future," Uncle George said, and he began to mention the splendid future of electricity or wireless telegraphy or of something else quite remarkable. But since Mr. Buttchenbacher isn't much interested in any future but the "future of retailing" that subject fizzled out.

Now comes the bad part.

Right out of the blue Pastor Needham said, "Well, Abigail, how do you like it out at the Smith Kenyons'?"

"All right," I said.

"My word, Abigail," Aunt Eunice said, "can't you stir up a little more enthusiasm? You should thank your lucky stars for the opportunity."

"Splendid family," boomed Pastor Needham.

Then Aunt Eunice offered him and Mr. B. more of her raisin pie. They each had another piece and said how good it was, which it is. And I've spent a lot of time trying to figure out what happened next.

There was this buzz of conversation what with Aunt Eunice talking about her pie and Mr. B. asking Uncle George about business, which wasn't the most tactful subject either. Business may be good at Mr. B.'s Emporium, but it's not at the hardware store.

I didn't think anybody was paying any attention to me when I started telling Joel about the baby, Willis, getting into the bookcase and how I needed eyes in back of my head.

Suddenly everybody shut up, and there I was saying right out loud, "I don't know why Mrs. Smith Kenyon doesn't stop having all these children unless she don't know how."

Uncle George choked on his pie, and Aunt Eunice got red in the face as a turkey gobbler and said, "Abigail, go to your room."

I dragged myself up to my room in absolute despair, thinking about how I always manage to get myself in trouble, opening my mouth when I should keep it shut.

It was too much to expect that anyone would forget, but they all started talking at once about something else as though they had. As I went upstairs, I heard Mr. Buttchenbacher say something about the Pritchetts and how old Mrs. Pritchett is looking for a hired girl again.

"Excellent woman," boomed Pastor Needham.

"Indeed," said Mr. B. "Nothing slapdash about her housekeeping . . . "

I shut the door and sat down on the edge of the bed, which Aunt Eunice always says not to do as it will break the mattress down and make it sag. I didn't much care if it sagged clear down to the floorboards right then. It would have matched my feelings exactly.

I was staring out the window at the dismal old rain drip down the roof of Daisy's barn when Aunt Eunice came up. When *she* sat down on the edge of the bed beside me, I knew she was really upset.

Her cheeks were all pink, and she said I must be careful not to make personal remarks about anybody. Then she asked if I had read *What Every Young Woman Should Know.*

"Most of it," I said.

I don't know if she really heard me or not. She looked down at her hands and said, "I expect you didn't understand it all. A person can make a lot of mistakes without knowing it. I've done it myself."

Then she told me to finish *What Every Young Woman Should Know* and said, "If you have any questions, come and ask me," which I would drop dead before I'd do.

Monday, March 13

While we were eating lunch today at school, I told Dolly what happened yesterday. Mary Margaret wasn't there for once. She's home with a sore throat.

"I was so *mortified!*" I said, and Dolly just *giggled.*

"You wouldn't laugh if it were you!" I said.

"I bet they had a perfect fit!"

"It was an awful personal thing to say, but it just popped right out of my mouth. I didn't expect anybody except Joel to hear . . . "

"Especially now," said Dolly.

"Why especially now?" I asked.

"Haven't you noticed how fat Mrs. Smith Kenyon is getting? Ma says come summer there'll be another little Smith Kenyon."

"My goodness!" I said. "That means there'll be *seven* of them!"

No wonder they all looked at me so funny. Aunt Eunice is right. When you're ignorant, you can certainly make frightful mistakes and not ever know unless a wall or something falls on you.

I wish I could fall in a hole or else leave town right now. There's not much hope of that unless Papa should suddenly decide to send for us, which he hasn't.

Come to think of it, I could probably open my mouth when I ought to keep it shut in California as easily as here. And I probably would.

Tuesday, March 14

I felt embarrassed to face Mrs. Smith Kenyon yesterday. I thought surely somebody would have told her what I said, but I needn't have worried.

When I got to the house after school, there were piles of clothes all over, on the ironing board, on the table, on all the beds, and Junior was dragging suitcases out from the attic storeroom. Mrs. Smith Kenyon set me to work right away packing.

She said she'd taken a notion to go see her folks in Kansas City. She'd be gone for two weeks over Easter. Junior and Myrna were the only ones in school, and they'd just have to make up what they missed.

"Daddy's ailing," she said, dabbing at her eyes.

"I'd feel awful if something should happen to him and I hadn't made the effort. He's been always there when I needed him."

"Yes, ma'am," I said as I folded up underwear, thinking about Papa and how he hadn't come home when Mama was sick.

She frowned then. I guess she remembered the same thing. "Well, now, Abby," she said, "I'm sure your daddy would help you if you really needed it."

"Yes, ma'am," I said again.

When Aunt Eunice heard that Mrs. Smith Kenyon was going to visit her folks, she sniffed and said, "Well, that's what comes of having a husband working for the railroad."

Then she told Uncle George they'd have to see to it that I didn't fritter away all the free time I was going to have with the Smith Kenyons out of town.

CHAPTER 14

Thursday, March 23

I have become a hired girl instead of a Mother's Help.

Uncle George and Aunt Eunice had what she calls a "discussion" about it, which Aunt Eunice won, so here I am working for the Pritchetts. It's just for ten days now while Mrs. Smith Kenyon is visiting her folks over Easter. Aunt Eunice says it won't hurt for me to miss school for a couple of days.

Aunt Eunice said I will learn to keep a proper house here, which I would never do at the Smith Kenyons'.

Uncle George said, "She'll learn to be a proper maid is what you mean. What will her father think?"

Then Aunt Eunice said, "I'd say he doesn't think much, not about his obligations. He hasn't sent one red cent for those children's keep. Unless Abigail can marry a Mr. John Jacob Astor, which hardly seems likely, she's going to have to learn how to earn her own living."

Uncle George started coughing. He says it's just a tickle in his throat, but it's worrisome to hear. When he got over the spell, he said, "Do as you think best, Eunice. I can't argue with you."

So that's how come I am here at the Pritchetts'. It did make me want to curl up and hide when Aunt Eunice started in about Papa. If I suit (and if Papa doesn't send for us), I may be coming out to work here this summer.

Mr. Pritchett came to town for supplies and for me, and we drove out to the farm in his wagon.

The Pritchetts have a nice house, but it's about eleven million miles from anywhere. The land here is as flat as a dinner plate with nothing much to rest your eyes on but the farm buildings and the clouds piled up off to the west, fluffy as white meringues.

I thought the Mr. Pritchett who came for me was pretty old, but it turns out he is Young Mr. Pritchett, the Pritchetts' bachelor son. He doesn't talk much, but maybe he doesn't have much chance since both Mr. and Mrs. Pritchett talk quite a lot.

When I first got here, I looked off to the west at that empty lonesome land. I thought about Papa out there somewhere . . . and Mama . . . and how we won't ever be together again, and all of a sudden I got this terrible sick feeling inside that made it hard to swallow or breathe, though I had to keep on swallowing and breathing anyway.

Mrs. Pritchett is very old. She has a picture of herself when she was young and you would not think it was the same lady. Her face has kind of fallen down, in fact she's kind of sagged all over, but she is a kindly lady.

All the Pritchetts are substantial-looking, square and solid like their house. They all look a lot alike, except that Mrs. Pritchett has more hair, though she keeps it skinned back real tight.

For supper last night there were big thick slices of ham, home canned green beans, biscuits with butter and honey, and afterward an apple pie twice as big as the ones Aunt Eunice makes for the whole family. But I didn't feel much like eating.

Mr. Pritchett said, "Eat up, Girlie." Then he told me I was skinny as a bird and they'd have to "fatten me up" and "put some meat on my bones."

Mrs. Pritchett calls me Abby, Mr. Pritchett calls me Girlie, and so far Young Mr. Pritchett doesn't call me anything at all. I thought being called Abby or Abigail was bad until Mr. P. started calling me Girlie, which is worse.

After supper Young Mr. Pritchett went off to a farm meeting. Mr. Pritchett sat in the kitchen with his feet in the oven while Mrs. P. took out her fancywork. She is crocheting a great huge tablecloth for Young Mr. Pritchett's bride whenever he gets one.

She gave a big sigh and said it was a great disappointment that here he was forty years old and still a bachelor. She says she can surely use some spry young legs around the place because she's so old and slowed down.

Mr. Pritchett said, "I hear Girlie here has a pretty sister. Maybe she'd be interested in an old bachelor."

Mrs. Pritchett said I was to pay Mr. P. no mind, that of course their Will was too old for Damaris. I didn't tell her about Mr. Buttchenbacher courting Damaris and being even older than their Will.

At eight o'clock Mr. Pritchett turned off the lamp, and we all went to bed. Mr. Pritchett said, "Us farmers have to get up with the chickens, Girlie," but I stayed awake a long time listening to the wind.

This is a very nice room. There are muslin curtains at the window, a rag rug on the floor, and on the bed a quilt done in about a million little bitty stitches and big, fat pillows filled with goose down.

It's a nice room, but I miss Damaris and Joel. I even miss Aunt Eunice.

Friday, March 24

I don't know what Mrs. Pritchett must have been like before she got so old and slowed down.

I thought we were going to run off our legs right down to our ankle bones cleaning house today though it didn't look a speck dirty to me, especially compared to the Smith Kenyons'.

Mrs. Pritchett says the kitchen floor (it's white pine) must be scrubbed with lye to get it properly clean. Fortunately she did it yesterday. I don't like having anything to do with lye since Joel told me I could go blind if I got a drop in my eye.

The morning just flew by, and then it was time for lunch. Mrs. Pritchett doesn't let me cook, which is probably just as well. I go for things and help clean up.

She says. "A man deserves a good hot meal after putting in a hard day's work."

And how they do eat. All that cooking, setting everything out just so on a clean cloth, and then Mr. P. gives thanks to the Lord (he should thank Mrs. P., too) and five minutes later it's all gone and all that's left is a pile of dirty dishes and some scraps for the chickens. Then before you know it, it's time to do it all over.

After supper I was so tired I could hardly see straight, but Mrs. Pritchett was still going strong. She kept saying how much easier we have it now than when she was a girl. And when *her* mama was a girl, they had to cook at a fireplace, make their own candles, and sew every stitch they wore by hand.

Monday, March 27

This was Wash Day. I never had to help with the wash before, so I didn't know how much work it is. Just thinking about all the sorting, soaking, and scrubbing, the boiling, rinsing, and wringing, the bluing and starching makes me tired.

When we were finally finished, Mrs. Pritchett looked at all those sheets and drawers and tea cloths flapping in the wind along with her outing flannel nightgowns and the two Mr. Pritchetts' overalls and said, "It's a pretty sight, isn't it?" She said it gave her a real sense of satisfaction.

It made me notice every drop of gravy the two Mr. Pritchetts dropped on the tablecloth at dinner.

Tuesday, March 28

This was Ironing Day. Mrs. Pritchett didn't trust me with anything ruffled. I did iron the sheets and pillowcases and the tablecloths and napkins.

"Iron them until they shine, Abby," Mrs. P. said.

We heated up the sad iron with the detachable handle on the stove and had to be real careful about it. I forgot once and the stove black stuck to the edges of the iron and came off on the lunch cloth so it had to be washed again.

Mr. Pritchett has come down with a bad cold. Mrs. Pritchett brewed up some special medicinal tea for him to drink.

Thursday, March 30

Mr. Pritchett sounds ever so much better. I asked what the tea was, thinking it might help that cough Uncle George has had since before Christmas.

"Girlie," said Mr. Pritchett, "you don't want to know. It's some unholy mess Aggie's grandma got off the Indians—blackberry roots, sarsaparilla, and such. Tastes a might like sheep-dip."

Then he went to the sideboard, got out a bottle of whiskey, and added a great big dollop to his cup. "This is what really does the trick," he said.

I was some disappointed as I'm sure Aunt Eunice would never allow whiskey in the house, but Mrs. Pritchett said, "Nonsense, Andrew. My grandma was famous for her medicinal teas, and she never used strong spirits in them."

She said to remind her before I go and she will send home a packet of her tea mixture for Uncle George. She says she's never known it to fail.

Mr. Pritchett said, "The teas don't fail, but sometimes the patients do." I think he was teasing again.

Sunday, April 2

A couple of Mrs. Pritchett's lady cousins came to visit this afternoon. Mrs. Pritchett calls them Sweet Bessie and Dear Alma, but as soon as the two Mr. Pritchetts saw the buggy stop out front, they left. They went straight out to the barn while Mrs. Pritchett sent me to the kitchen to make tea and set out gingerbread and raisin cookies.

For two such old ladies they certainly had good appetites. When I went out to the kitchen to refill the plates, one of the ladies, Dear Alma, the one with the strong chin with the wart on it, said, "I heard one of the Edwards girls was a beauty. It must be the sister. . . . "

A real expert on ugly, I thought, banging down the cake saver lid. It would have served her right if I spit on her gingerbread, but of course I didn't. Instead I gave her a skinny skimpy little piece and had the satisfaction of seeing her beady little eyes check the other plates with their nice fat slices. She looked at me suspiciously, but she didn't say anything, not right then.

"Thank you, dear," Mrs. Pritchett said with a smile. She told me I could read or draw after I took some cookies out to the two Mr. Pritchetts. As I was leaving, I heard her say, "Abby's a good-hearted child, Alma," which made me feel ashamed because it surely was a long way from the truth right then.

"John Edwards was such a handsome young man," Sweet Bessie, the soft-voiced lady, twittered. "We were all jealous when he married Emily. Poor Emily, passing so young. So sad for John . . . "

"Don't waste any sighs on John Edwards, Bessie," said Dear Alma. "He probably has Emily's successor all picked out already."

She just kept going on and on while Mrs. Pritchett tried to shush her and I whacked away at the gingerbread and thought angrily, how dare they talk about us, and about Papa remarrying? As though he would do such a thing. As though he could ever find somebody to take Mama's place!

The sky was a crisp, brittle blue and the sun bright, but the wind was as sharp as though it came straight down from the North Pole. It was too cold to sit outside, so after I delivered the cookies and gingerbread to the two Mr. Pritchetts, I took my book and sketch pad out to the glassed-in porch, where Mrs. Pritchett keeps her geraniums.

I couldn't draw or read, though, for thinking. Papa wouldn't marry anybody else, would he? And then there was that talk about Damaris.

People have always said Damaris was a real beauty. Papa did, too. I remember the time he brought her a blue velvet dress. He called her "his pretty princess." I looked in the mirror and wondered about me. When Mama saw me, she said not to worry, I was pretty enough, but I didn't believe her. I always thought she was just trying to make me feel good.

I heard the cousins start to leave and blinked back the tears. Once I start to bawling, I can't stop. It's like a fountain overflowed, so it's best not to start.

When they had finally gathered up their shawls and purses and gone on their way, Mrs. Pritchett hunted me up. I took up my pencil and started to sketch the geraniums as though I'd been drawing them all the time. She asked if I'd heard the ladies talk.

"Some," I admitted, keeping my eyes glued on my paper.

Then she said, "I'm sure your papa was very devoted to your mama, but people get lonesome. You wouldn't want your papa to go through life lonesome now would you, Abby?"

"No, ma'am," I said.

And I've tried to put what Dear Alma said out of my mind, but I can't. It stays there rubbing around like a rock in a shoe.

Tonight the wind came up and tore around the corners of the house. The thoughts still kept running around in my head like a bunch of squirrels. And all of a sudden I was crying so hard I had to bury my head in one of the big fat pillows so no one would hear me.

When I finally went to sleep, I dreamed of witches and wicked stepmothers, who all looked like Dear Alma and kept saying over and over, "It's a plain fact. She's no beauty."

CHAPTER 15

❦❦❦❦❦

Monday, April 3

Easter Sunday was real quiet with no kids around. Mr. Pritchett fell asleep in church. He said afterward that he wasn't asleep. He was just resting his eyes. I think he really was asleep, because he was making very peculiar noises until Mrs. Pritchett poked him with her elbow.

We had chicken for Easter dinner. I know it was chicken, but Mr. Pritchett asked me how I liked the "fried bunny."

Mrs. Pritchett said, "He's teasing, Abby. It's just chicken," but I couldn't eat a bite more for thinking of fried bunnies.

Mr. Pritchett brought me back to Estes today. Mrs. Pritchett hugged me and gave me packets of tea for Uncle George, and Mr. Pritchett paid me five dollars, which Aunt Eunice says is mighty generous. The Pritchetts were very kindly, but I'm glad to be home.

While I was gone, Joel quit school and started working at the railroad full-time. He's taking tickets and sweeping out the office. Joel says he'll be in the right spot when something better opens up, but Damaris is furious about his quitting school.

When I had a chance, I asked him if he thought Papa might get married again. Joel said he might all right.

"But he's so old," I said. Joel looked uncomfortable and said he didn't think that made any difference.

I didn't have to ask him if Mr. You Know Who was still seeing Damaris since he was sitting in the parlor with her right that very minute.

Tuesday, April 4

I now have a bank account!

Aunt Eunice surprised me today. When Mr. Pritchett paid me that five dollars, I thought I ought to give it all or most of it to Aunt Eunice for my keep.

She wouldn't hear of it. Instead she said it was time for me to open a bank account, that every girl should have a few pennies saved in her sock. After school she marched me down to the bank to show me how to open an account.

As we went in the front door, who should come out of the inner office with Mr. Grimes, the bank president, but Mr. Buttchenbacher. Mr. Grimes is fat and hairless and smiles a lot, at least he did at Mr. Buttchenbacher.

Mr. B. said "good day" to Aunt Eunice as he left.

Mr. Grimes said "good day" to us, too, but I don't believe he was thinking about us at all, not the way his eyes were glued to Mr. Buttchenbacher's back. Once outside he stopped to talk to Mr. Avery Trabert, Luke's uncle. He seemed to have quite a lot to say to him.

It really made me feel grown up to have money in the bank, but Damaris disappointed me. Here I thought she would be pleased, but when I showed her my bankbook she frowned and said, "You mustn't let working interfere with school."

"I don't," I said.

"Joel does," she said, "and Mama wouldn't like it one little bit."

"I'm not Joel!" I told her.

Sometimes it's a real pain how serious Damaris takes this business of being an older sister.

Wednesday, April 5

The little Smith Kenyons came back from Kansas City covered with spots. Not all of them. Just Junior and Myrna.

Today at lunch Mary Margaret kept asking when I was going back to work. Aunt Eunice won't let me go until the kids are better. She says it's probably the scarlet fever or measles, and she doesn't want me dragging it home to the little boys whatever it is.

As we were finishing up our sandwiches Dolly said, "Isn't it too bad Damaris can't afford to take lessons from Professor Vincent."

"Damaris sings fine right now. She doesn't need any lessons!" I bit down so hard I thought I'd broken a tooth, but I hadn't.

I was still feeling around my tooth with my tongue when Mary Margaret said, "Real singers, the ones who sing opera, are always taking lessons," as though Damaris isn't a real singer. That's when I got mad at her.

I guess I was really mad already. About Mary Margaret. I still wonder how Dolly can be best friends with her and me, too.

Thursday, April 6

The Smith Kenyons' house is quarantined. Nobody's

supposed to go in or out except Mr. Smith Kenyon until Dr. Raymond says the kids aren't contagious. So Damaris needn't worry about *me* working there and neglecting my schoolwork, not for a while anyway.

Dolly invited both Mary Margaret Vincent and me home with her after school to see her new silk party dress with the puffed sleeves and to have an apple turnover. Mrs. Raymond is famous for her apple turnovers.

On the way they started talking about the piano recital Professor Vincent's students are going to give.

"You can wear your new dress, Dolly," Mary Margaret said.

"I don't think I'm good enough to be in the program," Dolly said, and I couldn't figure out why she had such a funny look on her face.

"I didn't know you had a piano," I said, which turned out to be dumb remark number umpteen million and one.

"Her ma bought it from Mr. Buttchenbacher," Mary Margaret said, "the one your aunt Eunice sold him."

Then I knew it was Mama's piano, and I got this sour sickish taste in my throat.

Dolly looked at me a little anxiously and said, "I hope you don't mind, Abby."

"Might as well somebody get some good out of it." I looked down at the road and scuffed my shoes in the dust and pretended it didn't bother me a bit. I felt like running right on home, but when I saw Mary Margaret stare at me from under those pale yellow eyelashes, I knew that's what she wanted, so I smiled nicely and went along with them.

As Dolly opened the door, we heard Mrs. Raymond's little silver bell, the one she rings when she wants Bridget. The front hall was warm and smelled of apples and cinnamon.

Mrs. Raymond was doing needlepoint in the parlor. She turned her cheek for Dolly to kiss. She nodded to Mary Margaret, said hello and then, "We haven't seen much of you lately, Abigail."

"No, ma'am," I said.

Mary Margaret smiled (nastily) and said, "Abby's been out at the Pritchetts' farm working as a *maid!*"

"A hired girl," I said, sending Mary Margaret a *positively scorching* look. Aunt Eunice says there's nothing to be ashamed of about any honest work, but I had a hunch Dolly's ma didn't think the same, and I was right.

"Really?" Her eyebrows shot up about a mile. Her nose thinned out and twitched. Then she said, "I wonder that your uncle allows you to go out to service, Abigail."

Dolly wanted me to stay for supper, but Mrs. Raymond said she thought it best I go along home. I didn't mind. I was sure Mrs. Raymond's twitchy nose and eyebrows would spoil my appetite. Also my digestion.

When I got home, Joel was on the front porch. He took one look and said, "What's wrong, Abby?"

So I told him, "Mrs. Raymond looked at me as though she smelled something bad, like I wasn't good enough for Dolly, just because I worked for the Pritchetts."

"Maybe you're imagining things."

"I'm not."

"Come on, Abby," he said. "Let's go in."

"Mrs. Raymond makes Bridget Malone eat in the kitchen by herself, and then she rings that little silver bell for Bridget to come and clear off the dining room table. Mrs. Pritchett never did that. . . . "

Then he said, "How come you can't just laugh at Dolly's ma or use her in one of those stories you write?"

"She has Mama's piano," I said. "That's why!"

He didn't like that a speck better than I did. I could tell by his eyes. Just then Mr. Buttchenbacher pulled up in his new buggy to pick up Damaris. His hair looked freshly barbered, and he smelled of bay rum. He didn't pay us any mind, but when he came out with Damaris, he had a big smile on his face.

"Old Horse Teeth," muttered Joel as they left. Then he said, "Don't let Dolly's ma get you down, Abby."

"It's the piano," I said mournfully. "That bothers me something fierce! Damaris should have it. And Damaris shouldn't be spending so much time with Mr. Buttchenbacher either!"

"I don't know what we can do about it," he said.

"Papa could!" I said. "He ought to!"

"We can't make him. Cheer up, Chicken, someday I'll buy you a new piano, the biggest they make."

"You won't have to," I said as Aunt Eunice called us in. "I'll buy my own."

It made me feel better to talk to Joel, but I'm sorry I did. I think it made him feel bad. He was quiet all evening and went to bed early.

It's not that I mind about the piano for myself. I love to listen to music, but I never learned to play. Mama tried hard enough to teach me. As for singing, I can't.

When Aunt Eunice heard me complain once about not being able to sing, she said, "Count your blessings, Abigail."

"I try," I said. "But it's hard to count croaking like a frog a blessing."

"Nonsense," she said. "We all have to make do with what talents the Good Lord gave us and you have plenty to be thankful for. You have a fine, serviceable, speaking voice, Abigail."

Aunt Eunice made me feel some better, though I could have done without that word "serviceable." I'd rather be ornamental than serviceable. It's like the difference between being called a rose and a potato.

And I know what Aunt Eunice would say to that. You can't eat a rose.

I like being able to go to Dolly's after school (even if I have to see Mrs. Raymond), and my grades are improving, but I probably ought to try to find another job while the Smith Kenyons are sick. I wonder if I could work in the hardware store for Uncle George. Maybe he doesn't need any extra help, though. He let a clerk go while I was at the Pritchetts.

CHAPTER 16

❧❧❧❧❧

Monday, April 10

Something really nice happened today. Miss Johnson said right out in class in front of everybody that I had a natural talent for drawing. She had me to go into the primary room to show the little kids how to draw flowers!

After school I had to get right home. Aunt Eunice said instead of getting another job I should take care of the little boys three or four afternoons a week. That way she can help Uncle George down at the store.

On the way I got to thinking of things I'd rather do when I grow up, instead of being a Mother's Help. Maybe I can teach drawing . . . or draw pictures for children's books. I wasn't paying much attention to my feet and almost ran smack into Bridget Malone on her way to work at the Raymonds'.

As we walked along, I asked about Mrs. Raymond's silver bell. Bridget said she doesn't mind the bell or eating alone, which I could hardly believe!

"Sure now, I did mind some at first," she said, "but not now. It gives me thinking time, it does."

I love to hear Bridget talk, even though she didn't go all through school. Her voice has music in it.

As we passed the Emporium, Mr. Buttchenbacher drove up in his new buggy and his shiny new boots. He didn't pay us any mind but marched into the store like he owned the place, which of course he does.

"And have a look at himself, will you now," said Bridget. "Has the look of a courting man, does he not?" That made chills run up and down my spine as I thought I knew who he was courting.

"And will you be looking at those boots. I wonder if that widow lady from Cincinnati who's coming out to housekeep for him will be after doing them up."

"Widow lady?" That did make me perk up my ears.

"A cousin of sorts. The telegram was coming yesterday noon. My brother Tim delivered it. She'll have a time of it satisfying him, that's for sure."

"Have you worked for Mr. Buttchenbacher?"

"Not I, but my sister Mary did when his poor wife was dying, his second wife, that is."

"His second wife?" I'm sure my voice squeaked.

"Poor soul. There she was at death's door, and do you know what she was worrying herself over?"

"No," I said.

"The mister's boots and the four bushel baskets of peaches he'd brought home for her to preserve. And her with St. Peter's hand on her shoulder."

"His boots?" Joel says I'm awfully sensitive on the subject of boots, especially shiny ones, ever since I threw up all over Papa's.

"She always had to shine his boots even when Mary was there. He was that particular. Wanted them like glass so you could see your face in them like they was a couple of mirrors. He was never letting Mary touch them at all. It had to be the missus."

"Poor lady," I said.

"Not poor at all until she got married. It was *her* money that bought that fine store and her ever after with never a penny but what she had to ask himself for."

"I didn't know he was married *twice* before. . . . "

"It was before your time, I expect. Poor soul. Nobody saw much of her. The mister didn't hold with womenfolk gadding about, gossiping and such. Don't hold with music either, or so the poor lady told sister Mary." How awful, I thought, not to like music.

Then I asked, "How did she die? The second wife . . . "
Aunt Eunice doesn't hold with gossip either and neither
did Mama, but curiosity got the best of me.

"Well, now, that's a bit of a mystery. Fell, it's said,
down those stairs in that grand house. Lost a baby, too,
a boy child."

Bridget gave a large sigh. "Marriage is a chancy thing
at best," she said. Just then Luke Trabert rode by and
tipped his hat. Bridget's eyes went all dreamy. Reminded
me of Dolly and Mary Margaret Vincent when they talk
about boys.

"Handsome lad," said Bridget. "Sure, he'll probably
give his poor wife a bad time like all the rest, but he
is a fine-looking boy now, isn't he? Might make the
marrying almost be worthwhile. . . . "

Then she changed the subject completely and said,
"You'd not be knowing anyone needing a room, would
you, Miss Abigail? One of our boarders is leaving, and
we'll be wanting another."

I shook my head and wondered where there was room
for boarders in Bridget's house, which was even fuller of
children than Mrs. Smith Kenyon's.

"I'm thinking about that lady cousin," Bridget said,
switching subjects again. "I wonder if she'll be setting
her cap for Mr. Buttchenbacher."

I thought about her, too. Maybe I was worrying about
Damaris and Mr. B. for nothing. Just about then when
I started feeling better, Bridget had to go and spoil it.

"I expect the lady cousin is too old," she said as she turned down her street. "He'll be wanting a younger woman now."

When I told Damaris what Bridget said about marriage being a chancy business she said, "Bridget must have had some bad experiences. It doesn't mean there aren't good men around. Look at Uncle George and Papa."

"What about Mr. Buttchenbacher? Is he a good man, too?" I asked, thinking all the time that Damaris knows better than I do what kind of a man Papa is.

She only hesitated a second. Then she said, "He's much admired."

"So are lions and tigers, but you don't want to go and set up housekeeping with them," I said.

"How you do go on, Abby," she said. Then she went downstairs, her skirts swishing around her ankles and her hair piled on top of her head. Mostly now she looks and acts like a lady, but sometimes she reminds me of Myrna playing dress up in Mrs. Smith Kenyon's clothes.

Thursday, April 13

I didn't wait for Dolly after school. She's been so busy practicing for Professor Vincent's recital, I haven't seen much of her. For once I didn't mind. It was such a pretty day, the sky bright blue and the sun as warm as honey. Isn't that a nice-sounding word? I don't like honey much, but I like the word.

My jacket is getting tight around the chest, so I took it off. I would have liked to do the same to my shoes, but it wasn't quite warm enough for that.

The wind was soft and the air smelled of new grass and wild roses. I was thinking about my Amaryllis story and how a fairy child could ride the wind on a bit of thistle down when I heard Dolly call, "Yoo-hoo, Abby, wait for us!" as she and Mary Margaret came clattering up to me.

There sure are a lot of nosy people in this town. And one of the longest noses belongs to Mary Margaret!

I didn't know why they wanted to walk with me since it seemed at first all they were going to talk about was the recital and boys. Then Mary Margaret looked at me sideways and said, "What are you going to do when your uncle George and aunt Eunice move to Illinois?"

"Illinois?" That was where Aunt Eunice's folks lived, and she'd talked about visiting them, but how did Mary Margaret know?

"When they lose the hardware store—"

"They aren't going to lose the hardware store!"

"Of course they are," Mary Margaret said. "Everybody knows that!"

Dolly looked at me and said, "Don't worry, Abby. Ma says that that's not likely to happen even if your uncle is practically bankrupt. Not if Damaris marries Mr. Buttchenbacher. He'd surely charge less rent. He owns the building you know and—"

"Don't be ridiculous!" I snapped, giving them both a *perfectly withering* stare. "Damaris would *never* marry Mr. Buttchenbacher just to save Uncle George's business. And Uncle George wouldn't let her either."

"My goodness, Abigail Edwards," Dolly said. "You certainly have a terrible temper. My ma says if a girl ain't pretty and don't have money, she had certainly better be civil and genteel!"

She flounced off with Mary Margaret. I walked home alone, and I won't put down what I thought, but it wasn't civil or genteel, either.

Uncle George might not let Damaris marry Mr. B. to save his business, but I'm sure certain Aunt Eunice would.

The heroines in those books Dolly and Bridget Malone read are always making tragic mistakes and then are awfully miserable until the end of the book when the hero saves them.

The trouble is I'm afraid if Damaris makes a tragic mistake like marrying Mr. You Know Who, there won't be any hero to save her, and she'll be stuck shining his boots forever like his last poor wife did.

It was almost six o'clock when Damaris came home. I heard Aunt Eunice ask if *he* was going to call. *He* is. Then Damaris came upstairs. She looked tired as she poured water from the pitcher into the bowl and sponged off her face and neck.

Then she did up her hair again in a shimmering coil. I don't believe I will ever get the hang of doing that even if I practice for a million years. She dabbed her wrists and neck with lavender water and put on a fresh blouse. Making herself beautiful for that old man, I thought angrily.

"Are you going to marry Mr. Buttchenbacher, Damaris?" I said, as usual not keeping my mouth shut when I ought to.

"He hasn't asked me," she said, carefully buttoning up her collar.

"But you're thinking about it!" She didn't answer, so I blundered right on. "Just because Mama asked you to look out for Joel and me doesn't mean you have to marry Mr. Buttchenbacher on our account!" When she still didn't answer I said, "You think all our problems would be solved if only you married that old man!"

"Some would," she said quietly. "I must go down and help with dinner."

"He's been married twice already," I blurted out.

"I know," she said.

"What about Papa? What if he sends for us?"

"I'll think about that if he does," she said as she turned toward the door.

"He's got a widow lady, a cousin coming out from Cincinnati," I said, but she already knew that, too.

"His cousin Frieda," she said. "Karl is going to help her find a position."

"He doesn't like music either," I said. "He sold Mama's piano to Dolly's ma."

She didn't say anything for a minute, but I saw the little pulse twitch in her cheek. As she opened the door she said, "I must go down and help with dinner. You better come, too, Abby." And then with a half smile she added, "Don't frown so. Your face will grow that way."

She hadn't seemed a bit bothered about the cousin. Maybe Cousin Frieda is an old witch with a great wart on the end of her nose. All the same, if Damaris loved Mr. B., wouldn't she be a little bit jealous? I'm sure I would. I'd want to scratch her eyes out.

If she doesn't love him, maybe she won't marry him. She can't, I thought, pounding my pillow until it was squashed flat as pancake.

Later

Damaris isn't home yet, and I can't get to sleep.

Downstairs Uncle George is coughing. He never has gotten over that cold he took before Christmas, though he says it is some better since he started using Mrs. Pritchett's tea mixture.

Mama used to tell Aunt Eunice she was afraid somebody would marry Damaris "just for her looks, not caring for what's inside her."

Nobody ever worried that somebody might marry me just for my looks, not that I want to get married anyhow, ever.

I wonder what it would be like to have Papa or some-one call me Princess, though I don't suppose anyone ever will.

I keep thinking if anybody can keep Damaris from making a *tragic mistake* it's Papa.

Friday, April 14

Mary Margaret Vincent was right about one thing, though I hate to admit it. Aunt Eunice and Uncle George are thinking about going to Illinois. Aunt Eunice is anyway.

They had a "discussion" about it today. Aunt Eunice kept saying how it would be better for Uncle George's health if they moved, and he said, "I don't want to hear that kind of talk, Eunice." Then he started coughing so fierce it scared me to hear him.

Mrs. Pritchett's teas really do help him. As Aunt Eunice started to brew some up for him, she said, "If we do have to go, what will we do about those children?"

Uncle George looked up and saw me. He stopped coughing and said, "Take that worried look off your face, Abby. We won't leave you in the lurch."

"I expect we can go out to Papa," I said.

"And what would you use for ticket money, I'd like to know?" Aunt Eunice said.

"We've been saving. . . . "

"Pennies when you need dollars. And even if you had the tickets, it wouldn't be fitting for you to go, not without him sending for you." She frowned and sent me off to change out of my school clothes. As I climbed the stairs, I still heard the murmur of their voices. It's all very well for Uncle George to say not to worry, but what will happen to us if they move to Illinois?

Friday, April 21

Joel has become a hero!

He was hanging around the train yard after he swept out the station when an engine blew up and started a fire.

Mr. Trabert, that's Mr. Avery Trabert, Luke's uncle, got hit on the head with a chunk of metal and was lying there out cold. Joel was the one who pulled him out of the fire. Mr. Trabert would have been lying there burned to a crisp and dead as a doornail if it hadn't been for Joel.

Joel's eyebrows got all burned off and his hands are burned, too, but Dr. Raymond says he will be all right.

Aunt Eunice has been helping out at the store most afternoons, not, she says, that there is much business but somebody has to be there in case a customer with money in his pocket turns up. She came right home as soon as she heard Joel was hurt.

She covered his hands with goose grease and tore up

an old soft pillowcase for a bandage, all the time saying "if it isn't one thing it's sixteen others."

Joel is all right now, but it really scared me to see him with his hands bandaged and his eyebrows all singed off. I told him he just better not get himself hurt again!

"I don't plan to," he said, "but just what would you do if I did?"

"Disown you!" I said.

"Only Pa can do that." We were both quiet a minute then, thinking about Papa and him never being here when we need him. At least that's what I was thinking.

Saturday, April 22

Luke Trabert came to see Joel today. He says his uncle Avery is a very important man at the railroad and Joel will probably get a solid gold engraved watch for saving his life.

"You can't eat a watch," Aunt Eunice said as she took crusty brown loaves of bread out of the oven and set them on the table. "Let them cool a bit before you cut into them," she warned as she went out to the yard to settle a squabble between Dennis and Delbert, who were hollering bloody murder.

Joel said he'd be proud to have the watch. He has an old one of Papa's, but it doesn't work anymore. Damaris and I are already proud of Joel.

"At least this means you can go back to school," Damaris said.

"Only until my hands heal," he said. They glared at each other. The little gold lights in their eyes flashed like fire sparks.

"Don't fight," I said.

"I don't fight," said Damaris.

"Hah!" said Joel. "I bet Mr. Buttchenbacher doesn't know how bossy and bad tempered you are. Stubborn, too!"

At that Damaris stalked off, her nose in the air "like the Empress of Russia," Joel muttered.

I cut a piece of bread and took it up to the attic to eat. I wish Damaris and Joel wouldn't fight. It doesn't bother me when the little kids squabble, but I hate it when Joel and Damaris do.

CHAPTER 17

Monday, May 1

May Day. The little Smith Kenyons left a basket of flowers at the door. I heard them giggling in the bushes. They are all over the scarlet fever or whatever it was. Aunt Eunice says it couldn't have been scarlet fever or they wouldn't be over it so fast.

I have sent my letter to Papa. I told him about Joel being a hero, and then I wrote:

Everybody says Joel takes after you, being so bright, and Damaris says he must go on to school, but he wants to quit so as not to be a burden on Uncle George and Aunt Eunice, who are going bankrupt and thinking of moving to Illinois.

I stuck in a part here about Mr. Buttchenbacher and how Aunt Eunice keeps inviting him over for Sunday dinner and telling Damaris what a good catch he is and how he'd take care of us if only Damaris would marry him when he asks, which everyone says he is bound to do. Then I said:

Damaris is fearfully strong on duty. She says she respects Mr. Buttchenbacher, but I am afraid she will marry him just so we will have a fine house to live in and be able to go to school and not be a burden on Uncle George and Aunt Eunice and that she will be sorry all her life long if she does.

Mr. Buttchenbacher is awfully old, forty-five anyway, and he's been married twice before. Both those wives died. Everybody says he has plenty of money. I expect they are right because Mr. Grimes who owns the Estes Bank is always very polite to him. Joel calls him "Old Horse Face." That's because of his teeth.

Mr. Buttchenbacher has not asked her to marry him yet. I think if you would send for us, she would not marry him even if he asks her and even if she does respect him as she says.

We have been saving our money and we can mostly earn our own keep, but we need for you to say we can come. Aunt Eunice and Uncle George probably won't let us come, especially Damaris and me, without your permission.

Aunt Eunice has all sorts of rules for girls she doesn't have for boys. She says boys can take care of themselves better and not be "inveigled into a life of sin." So we need for you to say it's all right for us to come to save Damaris from making a terrible mistake.

Please write soon. It is very *important.*

Love, Abby

It was an awfully long letter and I had to write it over twice because I kept smearing the ink. I do wish my penmanship was as elegant as Damaris's. I finally managed to finish one copy with only one little blot, which is the one I sent.

Tuesday, May 2

Mrs. Smith Kenyon has not asked me to come back to work as a Mother's Help. Aunt Eunice says, "She probably needs you all right, but I expect Mr. Smith Kenyon has put his foot down now he has to pay rent on that big fancy house." It's not a fancy house, but it is big all right.

I do miss the spending money, but now that I have more time to study, my grades have improved. Aunt Eunice is surprised. She says I may make a scholar yet.

Thursday, May 4

Mr. B.'s Cousin Frieda doesn't have warts.

Dolly's ma saw her come in on the noon train from Kansas City and said she was "handsome and stylish" though she was dressed all in black, even her hat, which was only proper her being a widow. Uncle George saw her, too. "Nice-looking woman," he said.

"So I hear tell," said Aunt Eunice as she banged the stove lid down and Uncle George asked what ailed her.

"Nothing!" she said as she chopped up a piece of soup meat for dinner. Then she said, "It's a scandal, a single woman sharing the house with Karl Buttchenbacher!"

"The way I hear it, the poor woman doesn't have anyplace else to go, Eunice," Uncle George said.

"Poor woman indeed. No one who dresses the way she does is poor. Sarah Raymond said that hat came from Paris, France."

"I daresay Sarah would know."

Aunt Eunice kept whacking away with her cleaver. Then she said, "She'll be setting her cap for Karl."

It was a minute before he answered. Then he said, "It might be for the best, all things considered."

"How can you say that? If Damaris marries Karl, why we wouldn't have to worry about those children at all even if we have to go to Illinois. . . . "

Honestly! Aunt Eunice surely does have a one-track mind about Damaris and Mr. Buttchenbacher!

They are still thinking about moving. At least Aunt Eunice is. Uncle George sounded put out and told her he didn't want to hear anything more about Illinois, and Aunt Eunice said they might not have any choice.

Joel says business is purely awful, so that must be what she meant.

Friday, May 5

Damaris was sitting in the kitchen corner mending a tiny rent in her best blouse, and I was feeding beans into the coffee grinder. I was thinking what a lovely smell fresh ground coffee has when Aunt Eunice asked if Mr. B. was coming by. Isn't he always, I thought, grinding away.

Then she said as she took the grinder away from me and emptied it into the pot, "I don't know what the church would do without Karl Buttchenbacher. He pays a good part of Pastor Needham's salary, you know, and he has a fine voice, too. We must persuade him to sing in the choir."

"Karl doesn't hold with music," Damaris said, snipping off her thread.

Aunt Eunice looked at her sharply.

"Not even church music?"

"No."

"But he bought your mama's piano from me."

"And sold it," Damaris said.

"Whoever to?" Aunt Eunice said.

Well, I knew so I told her. "He sold it to Dolly Raymond's ma for a hundred dollars. That's how come Dolly is going to play in Professor Vincent's recital."

When Aunt Eunice told Uncle George about it later, she said, "He didn't pay us but fifty dollars, and he didn't even lay out cash but took it off the store rent. . . . "

She sounded put out. Maybe she's changing her mind about Mr. Buttchenbacher. Maybe she won't be so anxious for Damaris to marry him! I hope.

Monday, May 8

Mr. Buttchenbacher's cousin Frieda is gone. She came on Thursday and left today.

Aunt Eunice went around with a big smile when she heard. She said, "He certainly hustled her out of town. Nobody had a chance to say more than hello to her."

She was wrong about that. Mr. Buttchenbacher may have been quick to get her out of town, but Dolly's ma was quicker. Friday afternoon when I went home from school with Dolly, there sitting in the Raymond parlor drinking tea and nibbling sugar cookies was Cousin Frieda.

Mrs. Raymond shooed us out to the kitchen, but the pass through from the pantry was open a crack so we could hear what they said anyway while we had our cookies and milk. Uncle George says Mrs. Raymond would make a good spy, and that's the truth.

She started off asking little bitty questions, and pretty soon she practically had Cousin Frieda's whole entire life story, and it was pretty complicated. It turns out not only was she married to Mr. B.'s cousin, but also her sister was Mr. B.'s first wife!

Cousin Frieda said, "Some people thought Karl would marry me, but my sister Genevieve was of a . . . a malleable nature, easier to mold into a proper wife. And then of course . . . "

"Of course what, my dear?" Mrs. Raymond's voice was like honey, warm and sticky.

"One day I said to Genevieve, not meaning it, that I could never marry a man as serious as Karl. He overheard, unfortunately. . . . "

"He took offense?"

"He did indeed. And I'm afraid Karl never forgets or forgives an injury."

"But he's helping you now."

"Yes." She paused, and we heard the clink of her spoon against the thin china teacup. "It's been difficult to ask him for help, but I've had no choice. My husband left me very little. I do hope to earn my own way if Karl will only lend me the money to set up a millinery shop."

"Your hat is lovely," said Mrs. Raymond. And it was. A perfectly elegant mass of ribbons and rosettes.

"Thank you," said Cousin Frieda. "It is one of my own creations. Perhaps you will be kind enough to patronize my shop if Karl sees fit to help me. I'm not sure he approves of my little plan."

Mrs. Raymond said, "I'm sure he will approve. We do think a lot of Mr. Buttchenbacher here in Estes." Hah, I thought. I thought a lot of him, too, but I'd best not repeat it.

"This Edwards girl Karl is interested in . . . "

"Damaris?"

"Her family, they approve of this match?"

"Of course. It solves a problem for them. What to do with those children when they move."

"Is there no father?"

"There's a father all right, out in California."

"Is he not in a position to care for them?"

"It's hard to say. I understand he has a new position with a cotton mill, the Travers Cotton Mill."

There was a clink of teacups. Then Cousin Frieda said, "I did not know there were cotton mills in California. Where would this Travers Cotton Mill be?"

"In Oakland, across the bay from San Francisco."

"Karl has, how shall I say it? He has certain ideas— for the future—if he should marry this child. . . . "

"Damaris is hardly a child. . . . "

"Still she is very young. It does seem the father should know. . . . "

"If you ask me, John Edwards can thank his lucky stars if Damaris is lucky enough to marry Karl Buttchenbacher. Those children will be in good hands, I'm sure you agree."

I bit into my sugar cookie without tasting it. I did hate hearing Dolly's ma talk about us, but for the life of me, I couldn't stop listening.

"Karl is such a fine man, fine looking, too," Mrs. Raymond went on.

Dolly caught my eye, and we both started to giggle until we almost choked and had to go outside so they wouldn't hear.

"Fine looking!" gasped Dolly.

"Grown-up ladies do have some peculiar ideas of fine looking," I agreed.

"All the same I hope Mama buys me one of her hats," Dolly said. "The one she's wearing is perfectly gorgeous."

But no one will have a chance to patronize Cousin Frieda's millinery shop after all because she's gone.

Mr. Buttchenbacher brought her to church Sunday. He didn't look like he enjoyed it much. He kept swallowing stomach pills and glaring at everybody as though they were pitchforks, not pills. Cousin Frieda did look elegant. She had a big leghorn hat with miles of feathers on it.

Uncle George said, "Some poor ostrich gave his all for that hat," but all the ladies admired it a lot.

After services Mr. Buttchenbacher hustled Cousin Frieda into his buggy, and this morning she left on the nine A.M. train for Kansas City. Dolly's ma says she's going to work in a shop that sells French millinery.

Tuesday, May 9

Dolly doesn't have much time for me these days. She and Mary Margaret are too busy getting ready for the piano recital. I don't want to go over there anyway and hear Dolly banging away on Mama's piano.

Friday, May 12

Sunday is Damaris's birthday. She will be seventeen. I took a dollar out of my bank account to buy her a present. I think I will get her some Irish linen handkerchiefs or a lace collar. I wish there was someplace else I could go to get them besides Mr. You Know Who's Emporium. Joel says he is going to get her a new umbrella. He was going to get her some French perfume until he found out how much it cost.

Dolly fell and broke the little finger on her right hand. Bridget Malone had just waxed the floor in their front hall, and Dolly skidded on it. She stuck out her hand

and smashed her little finger on the stair rail. It has turned all spotted red and purple. Dr. Raymond put it in a splint.

I am sorry Dolly got hurt. It's probably awfully wicked of me to be a little bit glad she can't play in the recital after all, but Dolly says she's glad herself. She was getting very nervous about playing in front of an audience. Mary Margaret has been acting as though she broke her finger on purpose.

Sunday, May 14

Aunt Eunice baked a birthday cake for Damaris. Everybody liked it, especially Mr. B. Aunt Eunice says she likes a man to be a hearty eater. Mr. Buttchenbacher certainly is that all right.

Damaris liked the handkerchiefs. I don't think Mr. You Know Who gave her anything at all. He probably doesn't believe in birthday presents.

Later

I was wrong (again).

Mr. Buttchenbacher did give Damaris a present. An engagement ring. A big, ugly, old ring, one that belonged to his first wife. I don't think Damaris likes it, but she won't say. I don't know why she took it. It means she is going to have to go live in that awful old house.

It's not really awful, the house, only it will be if Damaris has to go live there, which she certainly will have to do if she marries Mr. Buttchenbacher. And she says Joel and I are to live there, too.

Aunt Eunice really surprised me. Here when I thought she could hardly wait to marry Damaris off, she said they ought to wait until Damaris is eighteen, but Mr. B. said, "Nonsense. Seventeen is plenty old enough." The wedding will be next month. Unless there is a miracle.

Why hasn't Papa answered my letter? Joel says he's written, too. He hasn't had an answer, either.

CHAPTER 18

꙳꙳꙳꙳꙳

Tuesday, May 16

Today I was so embarrassed!

I have been having an awful time keeping my mind on schoolwork, especially on the Civil War, which we are studying right now. I did manage to finish my report on time, but then I had to read it out loud in class and I said "mounted Calvary."

Behind me Mary Margaret Vincent started giggling her

silly head off. Then Miss Johnson asked her what I should have said, and she said "*cavalry*." (Which of course she knew.)

I felt myself get all hot and flustered and would have liked to drop right through the floor. When we were walking home, Mary Margaret said everybody knew Calvary was where Our Lord was crucified and that I didn't have to say "mounted" at all as *cavalry* means mounted troops.

"Thank you for telling me, Mary Margaret," I said as polite as I could manage.

I wish I could blame my mistake on thinking about the wedding, but I can't. I just always said Calvary when I was reading to myself and never had to say it out loud before.

When they finished teasing me, they started talking about the wedding. Dolly said, "Mary Margaret's mother sings for weddings. Maybe she'll sing for Damaris's."

I didn't know what to say. Once I heard Mrs. Vincent sing "Oh Promise Me." Once was enough. Joel says she almost sings it—she almost hits the notes before her voice cracks.

Finally I said, "I don't know if they'll have any music, seeing as Mr. Buttchenbacher doesn't approve of it."

Dolly sounded horrified. "They have to have music! Everyone will expect it!" she said. Actually Damaris sings much better than Mrs. Vincent, not that she's been singing much lately, but I guess you can't sing at your own wedding.

As if enough hadn't happened today, at dinner Uncle George said, "You haven't been writing anonymous letters have you, Abby? To your father?"

"No, of course not!" I felt a little guilty since I have written him, but I know I signed my name.

"Sure?"

I nodded. Joel and Damaris said they hadn't, either.

Uncle George said he thought not. He didn't say any more, so I don't know what that was all about.

Thursday, May 18

It's settled that Uncle George and Aunt Eunice will be moving to Illinois after the wedding but not until after school is out. Mr. B. has offered to take the store fixtures off their hands and to dispose of the stock and also their furniture. He's paid for the furniture already, but hasn't had it taken away. I don't know why he wants it, since he already has a house full.

"It's good of him to take it off our hands," Aunt Eunice said.

Uncle George looked gloomy. Then he said, "He's greasing the skids."

"Nonsense, George," Aunt Eunice said, but Mr. B. is making it real easy for them to leave.

Friday, May 19

When I got home from school, there was a whole pile of stuff in the back alley, a trunk with a broken lid, a baby carriage missing a wheel, and a box full of odds and ends: old shoes and clothes, a history of the Civil War with the cover gone. Delbert and Dennis were squabbling over Great-grandpa Lindstrom's GAR hat and cavalry boots. That's *cavalry* not *Calvary*.

Joel was in the kitchen buttering about half a loaf of bread. He said he needed nourishment to keep up his strength after hauling all that stuff down from the attic for Aunt Eunice. He said she was still up there "cleaning out the nail holes" getting ready to move and I was to go up directly after I changed out of my school clothes.

The attic was dim, dusty, and hot. I found Aunt Eunice lifting a dress out of Mama's old trunk. The muslin was cream colored and smelled of lavender.

"Your mama's wedding dress," she said. "If your hands are clean, take it down and lay it on the sewing machine. It ought to do for Damaris with a bit of altering."

I hugged it to me as I went downstairs, though I guess I shouldn't have, it being so old and fragile.

"Oh, Joel," I said, showing it to him, "what are we going to do about Damaris? If only we'd hear from Papa. He could change her mind. He's the only one."

"We have heard," Joel said, handing me an envelope addressed to us both. I started to smile until I saw the expression on his face.

The first thing Papa said was "honorable people don't write anonymous letters."

"I didn't! Did you, Joel?" He shook his head.

The second thing he told us was not to meddle. He said since Uncle George had no objection to the marriage, he didn't either and that he'd written as much to Mr. B.

Then he said, Uncle George's move was coming at an awkward time and under the circumstances he was grateful Damaris's future husband was willing to undertake responsibility for us. He said he hoped to be able to send for Joel and me when certain plans of his "came to fruition."

"Which will be never!" I said, angrily crumpling the letter into a ball. "He won't help!"

"Maybe he can't," Joel said.

"I don't believe he cares two pins for any of us. Damaris is going to make a horrible mistake, and he won't even try to save her!"

"It sounds like he's as hard up as Uncle George, Abby. Besides, maybe we've got it wrong. Maybe Damaris loves Mr. Buttchenbacher."

"She can't! She thinks we'll have a home and that she can get you to stay in school if she marries him!"

"She's wrong. I've told her I don't need her or Mr. Buttchenbacher to take care of me."

"So what can we do?"

"Nothing."

"Nothing?"

"If anything's to be done, Damaris must do it."

I said I wished she'd tell Mr. Buttchenbacher to go jump in the lake, but Joel said she wouldn't, and she didn't.

Instead Mr. Buttchenbacher and Damaris set the wedding date for June seventeenth, and Damaris says Joel and I are to move into Mr. B.'s house when Uncle George and Aunt Eunice go to Illinois. Joel says he won't, but she doesn't believe him.

Tuesday, May 23

I woke up in the middle of the night with what I thought was a *brilliant idea.*

Pastor Needham should talk to Damaris! Surely he would refuse to marry them if he knew she was just doing it so Joel and I will have a home and stay in school, which is why I think she is doing it.

I thought it was a brilliant idea, only it wasn't. Pastor kept his finger in his book the whole time I talked to him. He hemmed and hawed and said how it wasn't up to us to interfere between "a man and a maid," which sounded real ridiculous to me, but I expect it's somewhere in scripture.

Then he said, "Come now, Abigail. You mustn't be *jealous* of your sister's good fortune." And then he said I should pray about my attitude.

The sky was gray and there was the smell of rain in the air as I walked home. The weather matched my feelings. I sat down on the front stoop too discouraged to go in the house. It does seem as if Damaris is *doomed*.

About then I saw her. She was marching down the street a half step ahead of Luke Trabert with her nose in the air. As she turned up the walk, she said, "I'll thank you to mind your own business, Luke Trabert!" Then she snapped at me, "You'd better come in and help Aunt Eunice, Abigail."

"What made her so mad, Luke?" I said as the screen door banged shut behind her.

"I was just telling her Mr. Ames would give them a good price on wedding photographs. Then I asked about the music, and she about took my head off. Maybe her feet hurt from standing on them all day," Luke said.

"Maybe it's the wedding," I said, thinking it might have been his mentioning the music and Mr. Buttchenbacher not wanting any that upset her.

He sat down beside me and said in a gloomy voice, "Seems like that ought to be making her happy." I wondered if Dolly was right and he was sweet on Damaris.

"I bet if Papa was to send us train tickets there wouldn't be any old wedding!"

"You think that would change her mind?" he asked as drops of rain began to fall, making little splatting noises in the dust.

"For sure," I said, getting up to go in. "Not much chance of it, though. I expect it would take a miracle."

Damaris had rolled up her cuffs and put on an apron. She was setting out the silverware while Aunt Eunice dished up stew and gave her what for about Luke Trabert. She was saying, "You'd best not let that boy hang about."

"He comes to see Joel," Damaris said.

"Don't tell me that's all!" Aunt Eunice went on about how it would be plain foolish for Damaris to do anything to displease Mr. B. Then she did finally get around to asking what Luke actually said. Damaris looked her straight in the eye and told her.

"He said an honest man can't be as rich as Karl."

"Well, I never . . . " Aunt Eunice stopped with the ladle dripping stew and never even noticed. "So Luke Trabert thinks having money is some kind of a sin, does he? I suppose he'd like you to wait around for him until he makes enough to take care of you properly."

"Aunt Eunice!" Damaris's cheeks went all pink. She said Luke had never mentioned anything of the sort, but Aunt Eunice paid no attention.

"Or maybe he'd like you to traipse around the country after him while he's taking pictures. Your mama followed your daddy around for years, living in tents and drafty cabins, eating beans, and scrubbing clothes in cold water. Made her old before her time."

"She loved Papa," Damaris said.

"Much good it did her," said Aunt Eunice.

The stew tasted good, but Damaris just picked at her plate. So did Uncle George. Aunt Eunice kept looking from one to the other of them, the line between her eyes getting deeper all the time. She kept asking what ailed them, and they both said, "Nothing."

Later I said to Damaris, "I bet if Papa sent for us, you wouldn't marry Mr. Buttchenbacher." She just turned over in bed and wouldn't answer me.

Thursday, May 25

Aunt Eunice is still cleaning and packing. She says she would be ashamed to leave a dirty house for the next tenants.

Uncle George is not coughing so much, but he acts awful glum about leaving Estes. He says it's a fine thing if he's getting his health back too late to save his living.

Friday, May 26

Papa has written Uncle George and all of us.

He says he is expecting to be married shortly! To the widow lady named Mrs. Mary MacKay who owns the

Travers Cotton Mill, a ranch, and a house in San Francisco.

We all sat there for a minute stunned at the news. "Poleaxed," Uncle George said.

"Well," said Aunt Eunice. "There's no fool like an old fool." I stole a look at Damaris. She was frowning, but she didn't say anything. Neither did Joel.

"John's not so old, only forty-five," Uncle George said.

"He certainly sounds like he's plumped himself down in a tub full of butter—finding a rich woman to marry. So what does he say about Joel and Abigail? What's to be done with them?" she said, asking the question on the tip of my tongue.

"He's satisfied to leave the children here. . . . "

"That's taking the easy way," Aunt Eunice said as Uncle George tried to decipher Papa's curlicued writing.

"He doesn't want to interrupt their schooling, and"— here Uncle George stopped and peered at us over his reading glasses—"he says he's sure Abigail and Joel's concern about Mr. Buttchenbacher's age are 'unfounded.' He's written as much to Mr. Buttchenbacher."

Then Papa went on to say a man ought to be older than his wife, especially if she is a young woman such as Damaris who "would need the strength and guiding reins of an older man."

"So does a horse!" I muttered as I scrunched down in my chair, feeling sort of sick to my stomach. I tried to remember exactly what I wrote Papa. I don't know whether it was what I ate for supper that made me feel sick, thinking about Papa getting married, or whether I was worrying about what Papa wrote Mr. B. Papa surely wouldn't have repeated to him everything I wrote, would he? Surely he wouldn't. Not that bit about Mr. B. being so old and having horse teeth.

If I ever get over worrying about Damaris and about what I wrote, I guess I'll start worrying about having a stepmother.

CHAPTER 19

✤✤✤✤✤

Saturday, May 27

A letter came from Mrs. Mary MacKay, the lady Papa plans to marry. She said she is looking forward to our meeting but agrees with Papa that it's best not to uproot us at present. She sounds like a nice lady.

Aunt Eunice says "I hope she is, for all your sakes" and "Time will tell," as though she doesn't believe it could possibly be true.

Mrs. Pritchett told me I shouldn't want Papa to go through life lonely, so I am trying not to be selfish. I have made up my mind to like Mrs. MacKay if I ever get to meet her in person, even if she is taking Mama's place. It would be a lot easier if I didn't have to listen to Aunt Eunice.

"Anybody who takes on a house full of half-grown youngsters has their work cut out for them," she told Mrs. Smith Kenyon.

"I would have thought Mr. Edwards would send for Joel and Abby," Mrs. Smith Kenyon said.

"I bet he can't afford the tickets. He's working for this Mrs. MacKay he wants to marry. A ready-made family might upset the apple cart. John should be mighty grateful to Karl Buttchenbacher for taking on his responsibilities."

Sunday, May 28

Mr. Buttchenbacher doesn't like the new way Damaris has done her hair.

She put it up in curl papers, and it came out in ringlets all around her face. It looked real pretty, but when Mr. B. came to take her to church and saw her hair, his face got sort of stiff as though it was frozen and might crack if he smiled.

After services he and Pastor Needham came for dinner

(again). Mr. B. was still scowling. He ran his hand over the dining-room table like he owns it, which I guess he does as he has already paid Aunt Eunice for the furniture. She turned away as though she couldn't stand to watch. Aunt Eunice does hate to part with that table. She keeps it waxed and polished just so. We only use it on Sundays.

After the blessing, as the mashed potatoes and fricassee of chicken were being passed, they started talking about Pastor Needham's morning sermon, which was on sin.

"Vanity," said Mr. B., taking a big bite of chicken, and glaring at Damaris's curls, "is a Deadly Sin."

"Well, not precisely," said Pastor Needham, who then went on at length (great length) about ordinary sin and the Seven Deadly Ones.

When I went into the kitchen to help Aunt Eunice, Mr. B.'s voice and the words "painted Jezebels" followed me in from the dining room.

"Whatever ails Mr. Buttchenbacher?" Aunt Eunice said as she dished up more chicken and dumplings.

"He doesn't like Damaris's hair."

"Oh, that can't be. Damaris looks real pretty. I expect he's not feeling himself. . . . " Mr. Buttchenbacher may not have been himself, but it didn't spoil his appetite. There wasn't anything wrong with Pastor's, either.

Food seemed to improve Mr. B.'s disposition, though he still scowled whenever he looked at Damaris's curls. When the last crumb of apple pie was gone, he leaned back, unhooked the bottom button of his vest, and said he'd found buyers for Uncle George and Aunt Eunice's goods so they could leave for Illinois anytime they wished.

"Not until after the wedding," Aunt Eunice said. "We are so looking forward to the big day. . . . We had a letter from Damaris's father. He is pleased you will be looking after the children."

Mr. B. did not say anything in reply. But I didn't much like the look on his face. Not that I ever do.

After dinner when we were all sitting out on the veranda, Luke Trabert came by and said how pretty Damaris looked. Luke didn't stay. He'd come by to see Joel. Mr. B. watched them go, scowling as though he was mad enough to spit nails. Then he looked at me, hard, and I got this creepy feeling. He's never paid me much attention, and I'd just as soon he didn't start now.

I keep thinking about his cousin Frieda, how she told Dolly's ma that Mr. B. never forgets an injury. I sure hope Papa didn't tell him what I wrote about him being so old and having funny teeth and two wives already.

Tuesday, May 30, Decoration Day

Pastor Needham and Mr. Buttchenbacher made speeches about "our dead heroes and comrades who died in defense of their country in the late rebellion" and we all took flowers and little flags out to decorate the soldiers' graves. We put flowers on Mama's, too.

As I stood there twisting her ring on my finger, the opals changed color and seemed to catch fire in the sunlight. I know if Mama were here, she would think of a way to save Damaris from marrying Mr. Buttchenbacher. When I looked up, I saw Luke Trabert. Maybe, I thought, there was still a way.

"Luke," I said, catching up with him. "Your uncle Avery, he's an important man with the railroad, isn't he?"

"Sure is."

"Could I talk to him?"

"What about?"

I hesitated a minute, not wanting to look foolish or forward, but then I thought what harm could it do?

"You said the railroad might give Joel a gold watch as a reward for saving your uncle Avery's life."

"They probably will."

"I was thinking, maybe instead of a gold watch they would give him a pass, like the one the Smith Kenyons use. . . . "

"You plan to ask Uncle Avery for a pass . . . for all of you?"

"If we had a pass and it didn't cost anything for tickets, I bet Papa would let us come to California, and then Damaris wouldn't think she has to go and marry Mr. Buttchenbacher just to take care of our futures."

"I don't know. . . . "

"Maybe it wouldn't look right for me to ask," I said.

"It would probably be better if Joel did, but he won't. I know Joel. He doesn't like asking favors from anyone."

"Let me do it, Abby," Luke said. "I'll talk to Uncle Avery."

"Do you think there's a chance?"

"I don't see why not. He thinks a lot of Joel."

I don't dare say anything to anybody, but I've got all my fingers and toes crossed, and I've been so excited I can hardly breathe.

Maybe Damaris is *saved!* It would be a *miracle,* an honest to goodness *miracle!* I keep pinching myself as it seems to good to be true.

Wednesday, May 31

It was too good to be true.

Damaris is not saved.

Mr. Trabert told Luke he'd help Joel if he could. He doesn't much care for what he's heard about Mr. B.'s plans for us, but he doesn't have the authority to give out passes. Then he asked how come Papa wouldn't help. When Luke said he didn't know, Mr. Trabert offered to write to Papa himself, to tell him Joel was real bright and ought to go on to school.

"That ought to help, Abby. Maybe your father will send for you."

"Not likely," I said gloomily. "I've written. Joel and Damaris have written. Most everybody has written Papa, except Aunt Eunice. She thinks he doesn't have money for tickets, but thanks anyway."

"Sorry I wasn't more help."

"Those plans of Mr. Buttchenbacher, do you know what they are, Luke?"

"Uncle Avery didn't say," Luke said.

"Plans?" said Damaris coming to the door. "What plans are you talking about?"

Of course she found out what I'd been up to and was very put out with me. She doesn't want us asking favors any more than Joel does. And besides that, she said she has promised to marry Mr. B. and that's what she's going to do. She won't go back on her word. It wouldn't be the honorable thing to do.

I said she was being plain mule-headed, also dumb.

She said I could call her anything I wanted, but she wasn't going to break her promise to a man she respects.

Joel says we can't very well kidnap her and drag her off even if she is making a horrible mistake.

How can she even think of spending her whole entire life with Mr. Buttchenbacher? Maybe she does love him. Is respect the same as love?

Thursday, June 1

We were all in the parlor after supper when Mr. B. showed up. He's here all the time. If he doesn't come to take Damaris to prayer meeting or for a walk, he comes to sit all evening in the parlor. While he waited for Damaris to do her hair (she's stopped doing it up in curls), he sat there on Aunt Eunice's horsehair sofa silent as stone.

Aunt Eunice kept talking as though she didn't notice his bad mood. As Damaris came downstairs, she was saying, "I'm surprised you haven't heard yet from John. . . ."

"I heard from Mr. Edwards some time ago," he said.

"Oh, I'm glad. He's so pleased the children's future is secure. . . ."

Mr. Buttchenbacher looked at Joel and then at me. His eyes made me shiver. They were cold and black as the bottom of a well where the sun never reaches.

Damaris took a quick look at his face and said, "Is there something wrong, Karl?"

"We'll talk about it later," he said.

"But there is something wrong, isn't there?"

"This is not the time or the place, Damaris. I don't believe in discussing personal matters in front of others."

Damaris didn't say anything more, just pulled on her gloves and jabbed a hat pin through her summer straw, but there was a tight set to her mouth as she followed him out. He didn't so much as nod as he left.

"Well, I never . . . " Aunt Eunice said. "I don't know what's got into Karl Buttchenbacher," she said. "He wasn't even civil!"

"Now, Eunice," said Uncle George, "don't get your dander up. Maybe he and Damaris were about to have words."

"What's to have words about? We were just talking about John's letter. And then he up and leaves with Damaris without even a 'good evening.' "

"Maybe the man just has indigestion, Eunice," Uncle George said. Aunt Eunice said that might be so. He did take a lot of soda mint pills.

Aunt Eunice finally remembered to send the rest of us to bed. I didn't think it was indigestion bothering Mr. B. I thought he was mad, but what about? I couldn't sleep for thinking, so I slipped out of bed and down to the veranda.

The sky was so clear the stars sparkled like millions of diamonds on black velvet. I was thinking what a big empty old place the world is, when Joel sat down beside me.

Down the street came the clip-clopping of horses' hooves, Mr. Buttchenbacher's horses. When the buggy stopped in front of the house, Joel and I slunk back in the shadows and eavesdropped, as probably we shouldn't have.

Mr. B. was talking about Pastor Needham's message, which had been on Woman's Duty, when Damaris interrupted.

"Karl"—her voice carried clearly on the summer air—

"about Papa's letter, what did he say?"

"He offered his congratulations."

She was silent a minute. Then she said, "About Joel and Abby and their future . . . "

"Don't trouble your head about it, my dear. It's all been arranged."

"What's been arranged, Karl?" There was an edge to her voice. Maybe Mr. B. couldn't tell she was getting upset, but I surely could. "Don't you think you should consult me or Uncle George?"

"Your father has left the plans for their future entirely in my hands. He evidently shares my opinion of your uncle's general lack of competence."

I gasped. How dare he be so nasty about Uncle George? The porch light glittered on Joel's eyes, but he held on to my arm as though he was afraid I would go dashing out to smash Mr. Buttchenbacher right in the face.

"And what plans have you made for them, Karl?" Damaris asked. The edge in her voice was sharper.

"Joel's to be apprenticed to Mr. Ferris."

"To the blacksmith?"

"Quite so. And he'll be boarding with the Malones." The Malones, Bridget's family. How could Joel fit in that house? It was already jammed to the rafters with Malones.

"And Abby? What about Abby?" Damaris asked.

"Abigail will go to the Pritchetts' for the summer as planned." That wasn't so bad, I thought, letting my breath out slowly. I hadn't realized I was holding it.

"In the fall Mrs. Raymond tells me she is willing to train your sister—"

"Train her? As what?"

"As a maid. It's time Abigail earns her own living."

I could hardly breathe. For a minute all I could think of was Dolly's ma, her narrow pinched nose and her silver bell.

"And what about school?" Damaris asked.

"Both Joel and Abigail have had sufficient education for any foreseeable needs they might have."

"You can't mean that, Karl!"

"I seldom say what I do not mean."

"I thought they would live with us. . . . "

"That would be entirely unsuitable."

"But why? We agreed they would. . . . "

"Both Joel and Abigail have seen fit to write your father. Were you aware of that?"

"Yes." She sounded uncertain. She knew we wrote Papa, but she didn't know *what* we'd written.

"Both of them strongly disapprove of our marriage and have taken it upon themselves to save you from the Buttchenbacher ogre. I was among other things too old."

"Oh . . . " said Damaris with a sigh that sounded like air coming out of a pricked balloon. "They hurt your feelings, Karl. . . . "

Don't! I thought. Don't start feeling sorry for him!

"My feelings are not particularly tender," said Mr. Buttchenbacher. "However, I have never believed it possible for your brother and sister to live with us. Where you could have gotten such an idea, I do not know. And now, since I know they have no love for me, I certainly cannot ask them to live under my roof or eat food my money provides."

"I am sorry they hurt your feelings, Karl. When Mama died, she told us to look after one another. Joel and Abby were just trying to do that, however mistakenly."

"And is marrying me a way you, too, thought to watch out and provide for your unfortunate family?"

"No, Karl, you're wrong. . . . "

"I hope so, my dear." Then he squashed her to him until I thought he was going to engrave his vest buttons on her chest. And he kissed her, a hard, sloppy kiss.

"Don't," she said, pulling away, and I surely didn't blame her.

"And why not pray tell?"

"Karl, how can I marry you knowing how you feel about my family?"

"I did not plan on marrying your family. In fact, the less we see of them the better."

"Karl," she said slowly, "I can't . . . "

"Damaris, I warn you," he said in a voice that sent shivers up my spine, "don't say anything you'll regret."

"Karl," she began again, "I can't marry you knowing how you feel about my family. I'm sorry, truly sorry, please believe me."

He didn't say anything more. He didn't say good-night, good-bye, or anything. He didn't help her down, and he didn't come to the door.

Damaris walked slowly up the walk, and the screen door squeaked shut behind her. Beside me Joel whistled softly. Then as Damaris went in to talk to Uncle George and Aunt Eunice, we began to grin at each other like a couple of loons.

"He's done it," Joel said. "He's really gone and done it."

"Cooked his goose," I said happily.

But after I went back to bed, it was really stupid but I began to feel sorry for Mr. Buttchenbacher myself. I surely hoped Damaris wouldn't, not very much anyway.

I could hear her talking to Uncle George downstairs. When she came up, I didn't even pretend to be asleep but sat straight up and said, "You're not going to marry him, are you?"

"You were listening. You shouldn't have," she said as she took down her hair. It shimmered like dark gold in the lamplight.

"I bet he feels terrible."

"He may be relieved," she said, but I didn't believe it, not for one minute. She didn't look relieved either.

I lay awake until past midnight. Aunt Eunice and Uncle George were still talking in their room. Their voices carried well on the hot night air.

Uncle George was saying, " . . . I don't like Damaris working at the Emporium now."

"It will be a little embarrassing for her," Aunt Eunice said, "but I'm sure Karl can be trusted to behave correctly. That's the least of our worries. What are we going to do with those children? We can't just pack them off willy-nilly to John. He may have broken up with this Mrs. MacKay and taken off for Alaska or Timbuktu by now."

Uncle George said for her not to worry, that he was sure Papa wouldn't shirk his responsibilities. Their voices got all muffled then, and I couldn't hear anymore.

I hate being somebody's responsibility! Even Papa's. I heard Damaris turn over in her bed, but she didn't say anything so I don't know if she heard them or not. Sometimes it's hard to tell what she's thinking.

CHAPTER 20

❧❧❧❧❧

Friday, June 2

Damaris woke me up with her singing this morning. She was dressed and on her way to the Emporium before I got up, much less washed or made up my bed. As I went down to the kitchen for breakfast, I heard squeals and crows coming from the bedroom where Aunt Eunice was buttoning Dennis and Delbert into their rompers.

"Sounds like a bunch of birds around here this morning," Joel said as he poured milk over his cornmeal mush. "Happy ones except for you, Abby. Why the frown?"

"I stayed awake half the night worrying. . . . "

"Nothing keeps you awake half the night, Sis." Then he grinned and said he'd heard me *snore* clear downstairs. He was teasing. I *hope* he was teasing, anyway.

He said I ought to be most entirely satisfied now that Damaris wasn't going to marry Mr. B. Only he said "satified," teasing again because that is what I was supposed to have said when I was a mere infant.

"What are you worrying about now?" he asked, so I went over the list. Papa. Would he want us to go to California? Money for train tickets if he did. What to do if he didn't? Mr. Buttchenbacher . . .

"Mr. Buttchenbacher?"

"You don't suppose he'll try to get even somehow with Damaris, do you?" I asked.

"What can he do, Abby? This isn't the Middle Ages. He can't lock her up in a dungeon someplace. Don't go borrowing trouble."

"If we only had enough money, we could go out to Papa on our own. And even if he wasn't there, if he was off mining somewhere, or Mrs. MacKay didn't want us, why we could work. . . . "

"Aunt Eunice and Uncle George will never let you go, or Damaris either, unless Papa says it's all right. It's not like you're—"

"A boy! I suppose that's what you're going to say!"

"Well, a fellow can knock around more than a girl, and you know Mama told me to take care of you."

"She told us all to take care of each other! That's how Damaris got into this fix, trying to take care of us. I think Mama would tell us we ought be able to take care of our own selves!"

"We do mostly take care of ourselves. But we still have to look out for each other. And don't chew on your lip, Abby."

I stopped chewing, but I didn't stop thinking. "Joel," I said, "what if we were to stay right here in Estes after Aunt Eunice and Uncle George leave. We could work and rent a little house."

"A little chicken coop or a room at the Malones. That's about what we could afford."

"Well, maybe we could buy our tickets with what we've got saved in the bank . . . " I looked down at Mama's ring on my finger. The opals changed color as they caught the sunlight coming through the kitchen window.

"Or I could sell my ring," I said doubtfully. I didn't really think I could bear to part with it.

Just then of course Aunt Eunice popped into the kitchen. "Sell your mama's ring?" she said as she shooed the little boys out in the yard. "For train tickets? I should say not! And there's no need to get that stubborn look on your face, Abigail."

"But Damaris can't marry Mr. Buttchenbacher!" I do think I positively wailed.

"Of course she can't. Even if she wanted to, she's pretty well spoiled her chances." Aunt Eunice sighed. "No use crying over that lot of spilled milk. Damaris must give notice at the Emporium, and the three of you will have to go out to your father. It's about time he did his duty. I'm going down to send him a telegram right now, and we'll manage without your selling your mama's ring, Abby."

She pinned on her hat, told me to clean up the kitchen and to keep my eye on the kids until she came back. "If you're late to school, I'll give you a note," she added. Then she marched out of the house with a determined look on her face.

"You wouldn't have sold your ring anyway. No one could pry it off your finger with a crowbar!" Joel said.

"I'd sell it if I had to," I said. "What do you suppose she's going to tell Papa?"

"Wedding off. Kids arriving FOB . . . "

"FOB?"

"Free on board. Not including transportation charges."

"That makes it sound like he's being sent a sack of beans or something!"

"That's about what we are. A consignment of kids."

"Be serious, Joel!"

"I am. I expect Papa will come through with the ticket money, and you, Chicken, will be spending your next birthday in California!" With that he grabbed up a chunk of bread and left, banging the screen door behind him.

Why is it some people get called Princess and others Chicken? I sighed and leaned my elbows on the table since Aunt Eunice wasn't there to tell me not to. Then I dished up a bowl of cornmeal mush and thought of Mama and about everything that has happened since the last Fourth of July.

I was starting to feel blue, but about then Clay came in dragging Delbert, who was howling his head off. He'd run a sliver of wood through his finger. I had to sterilize a needle and remove the splinter. All the time Delbert was screaming bloody murder as though I was amputating an arm.

After I wiped off his dirt and tears, I had to clear up the kitchen. And all the time I was thinking about Damaris down at the Emporium and whether she should quit right away or wait until we hear from Papa. If we hear from him.

Friday night

Damaris didn't get a chance to quit. She got fired. If I were Damaris, I would be calling Mr. B. all kinds of names. She doesn't say anything about him, though even Aunt Eunice keeps saying she didn't think Mr. B. would "stoop to such a mean act of revenge."

I wasn't surprised *at all.*

She says she guesses it's lucky she's got the money in her pocket for the furniture. Mr. B. can't change his mind about buying it as he's already paid. Everything is still here, though. The dining room table is covered with papers full of all sorts of additions, subtractions, and crossings out. It has been for days.

When Aunt Eunice got over talking about Mr. B.'s "mean act of revenge," she called us in and told us what she and Uncle George have decided. With the money they get from the business and selling the rest of the furniture, she said, there will be enough to take care of their bills, which is very important to Uncle George, and for all our train fares.

"It doesn't seem right, your having to pay for our tickets," Damaris said. "We have some money saved. . . . "

"You'll be needing a bit in your pocket for your food on the train," Aunt Eunice said.

"But," Damaris went on, "I'm sure Papa will help."

For a wonder Aunt Eunice didn't make any remark about the unlikeliness of Papa doing anything of the sort. All she said was, "Your uncle says the ticket money is yours by rights. It comes to about what your mama's piano should have brought if Mr. Buttchenbacher paid cash for it instead of taking it off the store rent." She wouldn't listen to any more arguments, so I guess it's settled.

Saturday, June 3

This has not been what you call a good day.

The morning started off with Mrs. Smith Kenyon sending for Aunt Eunice's table and chairs. It turns out she has bought them off Mr. Buttchenbacher. Aunt Eunice had to let them go, but she wasn't one bit happy about it. She told Uncle George, "Those children will just ruin it!"

And they surely will. Their old table is covered with dabs of paint and has Junior Smith Kenyon's initials carved on top and tooth marks on the chair legs, probably Kevin's. I didn't say that to Aunt Eunice. She feels bad enough already. She's awfully attached to that table and chairs.

Then this afternoon a dray came (ordered by Mr. B.) to pick up the rest of the furniture, beds and all, and it looked as though we would be sleeping on the floor for a couple of weeks, since Aunt Eunice wants to stay in Estes until school lets out.

You wouldn't think things could get any worse. But they could. Later on this afternoon a notice came from the new owner of this house giving us three days to vacate the premises. The new owner is Mr. Buttchenbacher.

That was too much for Aunt Eunice. She stomped on down to the Emporium to talk to him (breathing fire, Uncle George says), but it was no use. Mr. B.'s left town, and nobody seems to know where he's gone.

Monday, June 5

We have been farmed out to kind neighbors until we leave. I am sleeping at Mrs. Smith Kenyon's. She says she loves Aunt Eunice's table. So far it still looks good, but then it's only been here a couple of days.

Dolly said I could stay at her house, but I don't feel comfortable with Mrs. Raymond since I know she expected me to be her maid. I don't think she really wanted me. That's why I stayed with Mrs. Smith Kenyon. I will miss Dolly, though, when we leave. We have promised to write each other faithfully and have exchanged locks of hair.

Mary Margaret Vincent said she'll miss me, too. I'm not sure I believe her, but she did say it. I don't believe I'll miss Mary Margaret, at least not very much.

When Mrs. Pritchett heard we were leaving, she sent Young Mr. Pritchett into town with fresh packets of tea for us to take with us. She said they would be good for whatever ailed us even in California and Illinois.

It's strange, but Uncle George seems to feel better. I asked him if it was Mrs. Pritchett's tea that cured him, and he said maybe, but then again maybe he was just too riled up (and mad at Mr. Buttchenbacher) to waste time being sick.

We have not yet heard from Papa. I know Aunt Eunice is worried. We all are. What will we do if he doesn't answer at all?

Friday June 9

A telegram finally came from Papa. It said, "Message

received. Notify S.F. arrival time." I guess that means he will meet us, or someone will.

I was disappointed. It seemed as though he should have said more. Maybe that he would be *happy* to meet us, but he didn't. He didn't even sound surprised.

Aunt Eunice said, "Well, what did you expect, Abby? An encyclopedia? After all, they charge for telegrams by the word."

He didn't send any ticket money. Aunt Eunice says not to worry. The furniture money will cover expenses. She has found a lady with four children who will be traveling on the same train who has promised to look out for us (not that we need looking out for, but there's no use arguing with Aunt Eunice about that). In return I am to act as a Mother's Help on the train. (Sigh) Damaris has promised to help.

Sunday, June 11

Today we went to church in Estes for the last time, and who should come driving up in a shiny new motor car (the first in town) but Mr. Buttchenbacher.

He wasn't alone. There seated beside him, all dressed up in an elegant gown, pearls and lavaliere, and a hat like flower garden with "rings and bracelets up to her elbows," as Aunt Eunice says, was Mr. Buttchenbacher's cousin Frieda.

Only she's not just his cousin Frieda anymore but the new (latest) Mrs. Buttchenbacher!!!

Aunt Eunice says Mr. B. is out to show Damaris what she's missing, which is not much I'd say, though Cousin Frieda looked happy and waved. Mr. B. stared right past us as though we weren't there, and then Aunt Eunice said she wondered if it was legal for them to be married, being cousins and all.

Uncle George asked if she planned to drag them up before the courts to find out, and she guessed she wouldn't. It was on their heads and they would be the ones that had to answer before the Judgment Seat. Uncle George said he was mighty relieved she felt that way.

Damaris has been awfully quiet. She hasn't said one word against Mr. Buttchenbacher all this time. She can't be sorry he married Cousin Frieda instead of her, can she? I'm afraid to ask.

Tuesday, June 13

Today we went out to the cemetery to leave flowers for Mama, and I got this awful lonesome old ache inside. Joel said something about coming back and putting up a proper stone for Mama, and all of a sudden I began to bawl. Damaris did, too. Uncle George hugged us and gave me his handkerchief when I couldn't find mine.

Somehow it seemed awful to go away and leave Mama,

but Damaris says we won't. She says we'll carry her right around here inside us for always. That made me feel some better.

Wednesday, June 14

Here we are California bound, Damaris and I in our brown serge traveling outfits. Damaris's is new, but mine is an old one of Aunt Eunice's. Joel's wearing a suit Luke Trabert gave him. Luke outgrew it, and it's a little tight for Joel, too.

Aunt Eunice, Uncle George, and the kids saw us to the train, and so did Dolly and Luke and Mr. Avery Trabert. Dolly and I cried buckets and promised to write.

Mrs. Smith Kenyon came bustling up to the station with all the little Smith Kenyons trailing along behind about ten minutes before we left. She handed Uncle George a letter the postman had left for him at her house.

"Almost slipped my mind, but like I always say, better late than never." She jiggled cheerfully all over as she laughed. After Uncle George read it, he tucked it in Damaris's pocket and told her to look it over later.

Junior Smith Kenyon gave me a packet of peppermints, and Myrna cried. Then she threw her arms around me and said, "You look all grown-up, Abby."

"Indeed she does," Mrs. Smith Kenyon said. "You'll have to call her Miss Abigail from now on."

"And we'll never ever find out what happened to the

fairy child Amaryllis," Myrna said with a *positively tragic sigh.* So of course I had to hug her and promise to send her the story when I finish it.

Mr. Avery Trabert told Joel if he ever needs a job he is to come back to Estes and talk to him personally. Luke said not to be surprised if he turns up in San Francisco one of these days.

Aunt Eunice was the one who really surprised me. She had kissed us all around, and then she told Mrs. Smith Kenyon she was going to miss us, especially *me.*

"Abigail," she said, "has turned out to be such a helpful child, she can come live with us if she doesn't get along with her new stepmama. . . . "

Joel winked at me. Later he said the prospect of living in Illinois with Aunt Eunice would probably make me get along with Papa's new wife even if she had a green complexion and warts.

"Aunt Eunice is all right," I said, and I was surprised myself that I really meant it, though I'm not sure I'd want to live with her again.

Then the train hooted, and we were all bawling and sniffling, and Aunt Eunice was telling us to be good, to write, and to be careful of strangers.

Uncle George handed up the lunch basket Aunt Eunice packed for us, which he said ought to see an army halfway to the coast, and Luke Trabert helped Damaris up the steps.

I was watching them and not paying attention to my own feet when I tripped. And I probably would have fallen flat on my face on the station platform and disgraced myself forever if Luke hadn't grabbed my arm.

"Watch out, *Princess*," he said, "or you'll break your neck."

Imagine that! Today someone thought I looked grown-up (even if it was only Myrna) and someone called *me* Princess, which I never thought *anyone* would ever do!

Then the train was moving, and we were waving goodbye. All of a sudden I thought of Mama smiling at me and saying, "Be careful of your wishes, Abby. They may come true."

Joel sat down across the aisle from us. He said I looked like the cat that fell into the bucket of cream and if I had whiskers I'd be licking them. Damaris had taken out the letter Uncle George had tucked in her pocket.

"Listen to this," she said. "It's from Papa. I guess he wrote it before he got Aunt Eunice's telegram. He says he got an unsigned letter that he thought at first was Abigail's work. . . . "

"I do not send anonymous letters!" And I do hate and despise being blamed for something I haven't done!

"The writer, whoever it was, said Karl was 'a harsh disciplinarian with plans for the children's future that border on indentured servitude.' "

"He had that right," said Joel.

"Papa says he discounted the letter, 'as the work of Abigail's lively imagination. . . . ' "

"The very idea!" I said.

"But a lot later he looked at it again, and it was from Kansas City, and so he didn't think it could be from Abby. Then he received a second letter from Mr. Avery Trabert, which he felt he couldn't ignore. . . . "

"Luke's uncle?" Joel said.

"Evidently he'd talked to Karl and became concerned about both your futures. Papa said he would have to leave it up to Uncle George to decide where you would be better off, in Estes or with him."

"So that's why Papa didn't seem surprised at Aunt Eunice's telegram," I said. "I don't suppose there was a return address on that letter, was there?"

The train started picking up speed. We passed the Smith Kenyons' place and then we were out on the edge of town with Mr. Buttchenbacher's house just ahead. Someone was on the veranda waving at us. It was Cousin Frieda.

"Let's see. He says the envelope came from a shop in Kansas City. A shop with a French name . . . Chapeaux de Paris."

Then I couldn't help it. The giggles started to fizz up inside me, and Joel said, "Let us in on the joke, Abby."

"I know who sent the letter."

"Who?"

"Cousin Frieda!"

I was just plain absolutely sure I was right. I remembered hearing she had a position in a Kansas City shop selling French millinery. Paris hats. Chapeaux de Paris.

"Why would she write Papa?" Joel asked.

"She wanted to marry Mr. Buttchenbacher herself! It almost seems—" I was going to say it almost seemed everybody in town had a hand in saving Damaris, but then I glanced at her face and stopped right smack in the middle of my sentence.

The train window was open and the wind was hot. It blew her hair into wisps and ringlets. She looked thoughtful, almost sad, and I had this tiny little twinge of doubt. She'd never said anything bad about Mr. Buttchenbacher, not one word, even after he'd shown his true colors (or horrid spots). What if she hadn't especially wanted to be saved?

"You aren't sorry, are you, Damaris," I said, "about not marrying Mr. Buttchenbacher?"

"Not a bit, Abby," she said with a smile.

"You don't mind about Cousin Frieda?"

"Not one little bit." Her eyes sparkled, and for a minute she looked about as young as Myrna. "I'm glad as a matter of fact. I hope they'll be very happy."

I leaned back much relieved and listened to the click clack of the wheels on the rails. I thought most likely Cousin Frieda was happy anyway.

There's a hot wind blowing and not a cloud in the

sky. The wheat fields are shimmering in the sunlight. We can't see them yet but somewhere up ahead are the mountains. Beyond them Papa is waiting for us. I'm sure everything is going to be all right. I don't know why I'm so sure, but somehow I am.

This book is almost full. Damaris says we must buy another one in San Francisco.